**"Are you, by any chance, trying to seduce me?"**

"It seemed like a good idea at the time," Emily said.

Kurt watched her for a moment. "And now?"

She sighed. "Now I wish I'd just walked in and kissed you. Then we wouldn't be having this nutty conversation."

His laugh was slightly strangled, but tender, and strangely sweet. "If I live to be a thousand, Emily Dawson, I'll never be able to predict what you'll do next."

She knew then. There were flaws in her feelings, but that's what made love real. She was in love with the last man on earth she should have wanted. The man who was in love with her sister.

Her sigh came from the depths of her heart. "Let's just forget I—"

But Kurt had crossed to her side of the bed, and was pulling her into his arms. He caught her and pressed her close to his body, kissing her so hard and deep, so *meant-to-be*, that her knees gave way. Her body flushed with heat, her skin tingling like a bad sunburn. But this wasn't bad.

This was very, *very* good.

## ABOUT THE AUTHOR

Karen Toller Whittenburg is a native Oklahoman and has lived in Tulsa for most of her life. She fell in love with books the moment she learned to read, and began to pursue a writing career in 1981. Taking a writing class convinced her that completing a book wasn't as easy as it sounded, but she persevered and sold her first book in 1983. She divides her nonwriting time between family responsibilities and working part-time as an executive secretary.

## Books by Karen Toller Whittenburg

### HARLEQUIN AMERICAN ROMANCE

### HARLEQUIN TEMPTATION

# How To Catch
# a Cowboy

## KAREN TOLLER WHITTENBURG

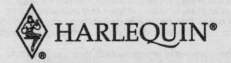

### HARLEQUIN®

TORONTO • NEW YORK • LONDON
AMSTERDAM • PARIS • SYDNEY • HAMBURG
STOCKHOLM • ATHENS • TOKYO • MILAN • MADRID
PRAGUE • WARSAW • BUDAPEST • AUCKLAND

ISBN 0-373-16772-5

HOW TO CATCH A COWBOY

Copyright © 1999 by Karen Toller Whittenburg.

**Printed in U.S.A.**

# Chapter One

"Hell, McCauley, you're too good for her." An emphatic nod of consensus made the rounds at the center table, and beer bottles clinked in agreement. "Too *dang* good for her, and that's the truth."

Through a haze of good buddies and good beer, Kurt McCauley checked the status of his broken heart and decided he'd felt worse. Two hours and several beers ago, he'd felt a whole lot worse. "She'll live to regret not marrying me," he said in another vague toast to the fickle nature of women in general and Carolina Dawson in particular.

"You betcha she will." Nellis Cohen slurred the statement into one long, vehement word. "Why, you're the most eligible bachelor in this here state of Nevada!"

"Damn straight! Plus, you're a gol'dern famous rodeo star," Sam Baxter said with greatly inebriated enthusiasm. "But I'm gonna tell you somethin'—

Carolina Dawson ain't the only cowbird in the clover.''

"She's the prettiest cowbird I ever laid eyes on." Kipp Trowbridge mourned the marriage of the belle of Fortune City. "Prettiest damn heifer this side of the Chisholm Trail. Prettiest filly ever to kick up her heels west of the Rocky Mountains. Prettiest little flower ever to—"

Nellis knocked the elbow props right out from under Kipp's melancholy chin. "You ain't helpin'."

Truth was, none of them were much help. Kurt didn't know why he'd let these hayseeds talk him into this commiserating binge, but he guessed their company, drunk as it was, beat the alternative. Melba, his Jack Russell terrier, had made it perfectly clear that she preferred to be the only female in his life. And as horses go, Hank was a dandy, but when it came to commiserating over a lost love, he just wasn't all that understanding. If he wanted sympathy—and Kurt was pretty sure he did—then these were the guys, and the whoop-it-up Silver Dollar Cowboy Saloon was the place. "She coulda waited for me, ya know." He held up his empty beer bottle and stared morosely at the slice of lime stuck in the neck. "She knew I always meant to come back and marry her. One day."

"'Course she knew." Sam whopped Kurt on the back and made a darn good effort to snap his fingers at the waitress. "Bring us another round, will ya, darlin'?"

The waitress sashayed over to the table, eyeing Kurt with interest. "Hey, I saw you on the news. You're the guy who trained that horse in that movie." She frowned with the effort of remembering. "Oh, jeez, what *was* the name of that movie?"

"Which one?" Steve Cooper drawled with a know-it-all slur. "Hell, honey, this guy's on call twenty-four-seven with those movie and television people. He's even got a dog that's got her own sitcom on the TV. Why, my friend here is only the best damn animal handler this side of Istanbul!"

"Wow," said the waitress. "I never met a movie star before."

Kurt shifted uncomfortably under her wide-eyed stare. "I just train the animals," he said, tipping his empty bottle to his lips as a diversion.

"Get the man another beer, darlin'," Sam said. "Cain't you see he's nursin' a broken heart?"

Reaching for Kurt's bottle, the waitress let her breasts brush his arm. Sensually. Purposefully. Again. "I have a surefire cure for what ails you, honey," she said, and smiled, up-close and personal.

Kurt thought he smiled back. He meant to, but Sam whopped him on the back again and let out a whoop. "What'd I tell ya? Women *want* you, man!"

From across the table, Max Thurman belched before adding his two-cents worth. "Carolina Dawson ain't the only woman in the world, McCauley. There's plenty of 'em out there just waitin' for a lonesome cowboy like you to come along.''

Nellis thumped his bottle against the wooden tabletop. ''You ain't just whistlin' Dixie, my friend. Why, there must be hundreds of women who'd've waited until hell froze over to marry Kurt, ain't that right, boys?''

''Yes, sirree, bob!''

''Hun'erds of women!''

''Thousands!''

''Heck fire, there mus' be a *million* of 'em out there! You're *famous*, McCauley. All you gotta do is say the word and every woman in this bar'll be standin' in line to marry you afore midnight tonight!''

The boys made another round of beer bottle clinks, congratulating themselves on their insights and their camaraderie. Kurt eyed the fresh beer bottle sitting on the table before him, a twist of lime cracked across its rim, its surface slick with condensation, its contents fizzing with the elixir of forgetfulness. He knew he'd had too much already, knew he ought to quit now, cash in the evening as a lost cause and go home. But then it wasn't every day a man found out the woman he'd intended to marry had up and married someone else. The way Kurt figured it, he owed himself one ripsnorter of a night in homage to all the marital bliss he was never going to have.

Heck, he owed it to every mother's son in Fortune City. There wasn't one of them, young or old, who hadn't been in love with Carolina Dawson at one time or another. There wasn't one of them, hitched or not, who wouldn't have jumped at the chance to marry her. But Kurt was the only one of them who'd ever had a prayer. Kurt was the one she wanted.

Had wanted.

He picked up the beer bottle and slugged back twelve more ounces.

NORMALLY, Emily Dawson steered clear of the Silver Dollar Cowboy Saloon and its clientele. She didn't like the stale, smoky air inside the bar, and she didn't like the country songs that whined, one after another, out of the jukebox. Her opinion of the men who frequented the Silver Dollar wasn't high, and even if she had wanted a drink—which she didn't—this bar would rank, in order of preference, only slightly higher than sharing a jug of rotgut moonshine in a drainage ditch.

But she was no fool. In a town the size of Fortune City, there was only one place to go if you were looking for trouble. Sure enough, the moment she walked through the murky entrance, Emily saw him and knew the rumors were true. Kurt McCauley, the bane of her otherwise pleasant existence, the fly in the ointment of her success, had come home.

"Hey, Emily, over here." Mary Lynn Perkins waved her to join the group of girlfriends sitting two tables away from the door. The other three women at the table glanced up in greeting, then shuffled their chairs to make an extra place.

"Hi," Emily said as she pulled up a vacant chair and filled the empty space. "Have I missed anything?"

"Just the preliminary roundup." Genna Bates scooted her chair a quarter turn so she could keep an eye on the mavericks who occupied the center of the room and the center of attention. "So far, the herd has been unexpectedly docile."

"They're getting restless, though." Jeannie Gibson lifted her brimming mug in a gesture of welcome. "The gunfight could start any minute now."

Renetta Zaltoski's big brown eyes widened, it being her first time at the Silver Dollar and all. "They're going to start shooting?"

"Shooting off their mouths," Emily said dryly. "If they hold true to form, they'll do something incredibly dumb, we'll have a good laugh, and then everyone will go home."

"They appear to be getting pretty drunk," Renetta observed.

Mary Lynn met Emily's eyes across the table. "That's where the incredibly dumb part comes in.

When these guys find an excuse to get together like this, they don't have a lick of sense to share among them."

"Fortunately, they only do this about once a year," Genna said. "Which is about as often as I care to come out to this smoke hole and watch them make complete jerks of themselves."

"Oh, but usually Kurt's not with them, and you have to admit he's worth the trip." Jeannie turned to Renetta. "It's been a long time since Kurt darkened the swinging doors of this saloon. We haven't seen much of him the last several years, but the rest of these local yokels occasionally manage to keep us entertained." She laughed. "The last time they got this drunk, Nellis wound up in Nova Scotia."

"And the funny part was they actually thought they'd put him on a plane to Scottsdale." Genna shook her head, setting her red-gold curls bouncing. "We found out later that the idiot had changed planes *twice* without ever noticing he wasn't in Arizona."

"If any one of them had a brain, they'd be dangerous." Emily ordered a ginger ale and settled in to observe the back of Kurt McCauley's dark head. If he had a brain, he'd have taken her up on her business offer six months ago, and they'd both be in tall cotton now. She was sorry that she'd ever wasted a minute following his not always illustrious career. But when he'd left Fortune City, she couldn't help scanning the newspapers and rodeo magazines for his name and reading—with an embarrassing degree of fascination—the accounts of the daredevil stunts that had catapulted him from the rodeo circuit to Hollywood. Her idea of using his name to promote the line of Western wear she'd developed was brilliant. Kurt hadn't agreed, which only proved that fame hadn't changed him in the slightest. He was still an idiot. As far as Emily was concerned, a broken heart was none too good for him.

"Which one was engaged to your sister?" Renetta craned her neck to see around the short-skirted cowgirl who stood between their table and a clear view of the men.

Emily narrowed her eyes on Kurt. "The one who keeps getting slapped on the back. His name is Kurt McCauley, but he and Carolina were never engaged. They've had an on-again, off-again relationship practically since grade school. I guess most people expected them to get married, but there was nothing official about it."

"Really," Renetta said curiously. "Then how come he's taking her marriage so hard?"

Emily shrugged, but couldn't pull her gaze away from Kurt's melancholy smile. She couldn't stop the squeeze that tightened across her chest, either, although she was determined not to let it happen again. She could count the number of times Kurt had been nice to her on one hand, and the fact that he'd been one of only a handful of people who'd encouraged her to open her Western wear store couldn't overshadow the many times he'd teased and aggravated her.

Kurt lurched to his feet suddenly, but was pulled back to his chair on a wave of laughter. A second later, to the ribald encouragement of the Corona poster boys, he was tossing back another beer. His neck was long and lean, his skin tanned and supple as he tipped his head to accommodate the ale he poured down his throat. He was in need of a haircut, and when his head was back, several dark strands crossed his shirt collar in uneven tags. There was a faint wave in his hair where his hat rode, and the hint of a curl just behind his ear. His mustache was too thick by half, and if Emily had had any opinion at all regarding his appearance—which she definitely did not—she'd have wanted to take a buzz saw to his upper lip. He was disgustingly handsome…and the Dawson family was well rid of him.

"Lord love a bug, he is *fine*." Renetta dropped her chin onto her hands while she admired Kurt's profile. "Your sister must be crazy."

"No, she's not," Emily said. Self-centered? Self-absorbed? Selfish? Yes. Yes. Yes. But crazy? Oh, no, not by a long shot. Emily suspected, despite years of evidence to the contrary, that Kurt had never really been in love with her sister. And she knew that, on some level, Carolina must have suspected it, too.

"Well, she certainly overplayed her hand this time around," Jeannie said. "I'll bet she'll kick herself sideways to Sunday when she finds out Kurt came home not two weeks after she got married."

Genna nodded agreement. "She shouldn't have given up on him so soon."

Mary Lynn chose a pretzel from the snack bowl, popped it into her mouth and crunched aggressively. "Oh, *poor* Carolina," she crooned. "While she's honeymooning in the Caribbean with her Brooks Brothers husband, every cowpoke in this one-horse town is getting drunk in her honor. It must be just *terrible* for her to know a man like Kurt McCauley can't *bear* the thought that she's no longer single. Well, I say goodbye and good riddance, Carolina! I'll be only too happy to soothe Kurt's broken heart."

Emily frowned at her. "Give me a break, Mary Lynn. You don't want Kurt McCauley."

Mary Lynn nodded. "I do. Oh, yes, I do."

"Get in line." Genna sipped her beer and stared longingly at Kurt. "That man was made in heaven for me."

Emily turned to reassure Renetta. "They're joking."

"Don't you believe it for a second," Mary Lynn

countered. "We never joke when it comes to men. Isn't that right, Jeannie?"

Jeannie, stalwart and unimpressionable, got a dreamy look in her eyes. "I don't want the man forever, you understand, but a few nights with him...well, I think it could change my whole attitude, help me lose a few pounds, exercise more, eat healthier. There's no telling how much good that man could do for me." Her cheeky grin returned to Emily. "We know you think he's a lower life-form, Em, but frankly, my dear, we don't give a damn."

"That's right," Genna added. "The fact that you wouldn't take him if he was a blank check is better for us, anyhow. One less female to shove out of the way."

Emily lifted her glass in a pensive salute. "You guys are sick, but hey, it's a free country. Have at him."

"Don't you like him?" Renetta asked. "I mean, if he was almost your brother-in-law, you must know him pretty well."

"He's trouble," Emily said, summing up in two words what she'd figured out the first time Kurt McCauley had ever actually acknowledged her existence. She'd been a gawky eleven, he a strapping seventeen. He'd tied her ponytail in a knot. She'd stuck out her tongue and called him a stupid peanut. Their relationship had pretty much gone downhill from there. "If you're smart, Renetta, you'll ignore him and the ravings of the lunatics sitting at this table. What any woman sees in him just flat escapes me.''

"Jeez, Emily, open those baby browns," Genna suggested with a sort of low groan. "Kurt McCauley is so good-looking it nearly puts your eyes out. He's built like a Porsche, sleek, full-bodied, exotic trim, all luxurious power from top to bottom and—''

"—and what a bottom it is, too," Jeannie added.

"Oh, yeah," Mary Lynn crooned her agreement. "Sex with him would be like…like…''

"Like a ten-second ride on a bucking bronc.'' Emily inserted a bit of reality into their fantasy. "With a fast, hard fall afterward.'' She warned Renetta with a he's-not-worth-it arch of her brows. "I'm not denying that the man is attractive. And I'm not saying that he can't be charming when he wants to be. But he's hardheaded and wild at heart, and most likely to stay that way…forever and ever, amen. Trust me, he's not worth the trouble.''

"He doesn't look hardheaded." Renetta continued to stare wistfully at Kurt. "Maybe a little wild.''

"A wild heart," Genna agreed with a long sigh. "Which makes the chase so much more exciting.''

Emily shook her head, sure the fun was in teasing her as much as in contemplating any real involvement with Kurt. With the exception of Renetta, these women had watched Kurt over the years, same as Emily had. They knew the easy way he fell into trouble and the ease with which he could explain it away. His good looks and fiery smile had gotten him out of as many scrapes as ever they'd gotten him into. Maybe people felt sorry for him because his mother had died when he was just a boy and he'd lost his dad a month before high school graduation, but no one in town ever believed Kurt meant any mischief. He was just full of sauce, a phrase uttered often and aptly about ''that McCauley boy.''

It was Emily's considered opinion that Kurt had been born under a wandering star and she, for one, wasn't surprised when he'd hit the road. With barely any goodbyes, Kurt had left Fortune City behind, first for the rodeo circuit, later for a roundabout route through college—God only knew how he'd managed to get in, much less graduate—and afterward, a series of careers that never quite seemed to satisfy him. Emily liked to think she'd have forgotten all about him if he'd just stayed gone. But he kept coming back. Back to Fortune City. Back to the ramshackle ranch one McCauley or another had called home for nearly a hundred years. Back to Carolina Dawson.

Renetta watched the men thoughtfully as she munched on a pretzel. ''He looks pretty heartbroken to me, too. Maybe he really did want to marry your sister.''

''Oh, there's no doubt about it.'' Jeannie tossed back a handful of sesame sticks. ''He always *meant* to marry Carolina. Everyone thought so. She just got tired of waiting.''

Emily looked at Kurt, trying to discern whether his heartache was genuine or just a good reason to gather his buddies for a grand, welcome-home, let's-get-drunk reunion. She'd never understood why Carolina put up with his lackadaisical attention. Unless it was the sheer novelty of having any male treat her as if she were—*gasp*—ordinary. Emily, on the other hand, was accustomed to opening doors for herself and spending a Saturday night at home waiting for the phone call that never came. But Carolina? Oh, no. Men fell all over themselves trying to please her, and consequently, Kurt's on-again, off-again attention had worked like a magnet, winning Carolina's heart a dozen times over.

Another round of rowdiness raised the decibel level in the bar as Cooper clambered onto the table, wobbled manfully and still managed to spill not a drop of his beer. "I got an an—annout—cense.'' He laughed loudly, too inebriated to know, or care, how drunk he really was. "I got som'phun' to say.'' He waved his arms like a maestro until the hubbub died down. "Ya'll know my good buddy, Kurt, here.'' Steve gestured at his good buddy and nearly fell off the table. He recovered his balance, grinning like a fool. "Well, ol' Kurt, here—'' he gestured and wobbled some more "—has just lost the woman he loved more'n he loves his horse, Hank.'' There was a general sad murmur of commiseration from the men. "So," Steve continued. "It's our oblah... oblah...*duty* as his sworn pals to prove beyond a rea—reashonable doubt that there's plenty a' women who'd be more'n grateful to marry a fine, up... upstandin' man like hisself." Steve looked to the nodding heads for backup.

The nods continued until Nellis bellowed, "Kurt don't care who he marries!"

"Yeah! He don't care that he got ji—*jilted.*" Max Thurman had a booming voice and sounded like he knew whereof he spoke...once he figured out what he was saying.

"Plenny of women!" Kipp Trowbridge struck the table so hard, his fist bounced back and he hit himself square on the forehead. "Ow," he said.

Steve shushed the men with a sweeping, beer-bottle gesture. "So here's what we're gonna do. We're gonna have us a cowboy raffle!"

The men cheered, stomping their feet and whooping like it was payday. Over the din, Mary Lynn yelled across the table. "Did he say they're going to *wrestle?*"

"There's no way those idiots can wrestle in here and not tear the place down," Genna observed.

"The owner isn't going to let them wreck his bar," Renetta said, clearly intrigued by the prospect.

"Raffle," Jeannie clarified above the hoopla. "They're going to *raffle* a cowboy."

"Now, what Einstein thought of that brilliant idea?" Emily wondered aloud. "As if drunken cowboys are so hard to come by, we'd need a raffle ticket to get one."

"I suppose it depends on the cowboy," Mary Lynn said. "And, uh, what you wanted to do with him."

"Mary Lynn Perkins, don't tell me you're thinking you could take Kurt McCauley home with you and that you'd plunk down your hard-earned money to do it."

Mary Lynn shrugged. "I really didn't work that hard to earn this money."

"I'm in," Genna declared. "Winning Kurt in a raffle would be a shot in the arm to my social life."

"You have to set higher goals for yourself, Gen." Emily patted her friend's hand. "Having Kurt dead drunk on your couch would be more like a vaccination than a social life."

Genna made a face. "No one can say for sure *when* he'll pass out, and afterward, I'll be able to say I've had him in my bed...which will improve my fantasy life, if nothing else."

"Hey, I just thought of something." Jeannie brightened with a new idea. "If you win a quilt in a raffle, nobody makes you give it back the next day. It's yours to keep as long as you want."

Mary Lynn's smile went wide. "Kurt McCauley

will *belong,* body and soul—well, body, anyway—
to whoever holds that winning ticket.''

Renetta grabbed her purse. "I'm buying a
dozen.''

"Don't be silly," Emily said reasonably. "It's a
joke. An incredibly dumb joke. And even if it
wasn't, these guys are plastered. They might decide
to charge fifty bucks a chance, or substitute Nellis
for Kurt.''

"Hmm." Jeannie pulled out her wallet. "You
think they'll take a credit card?''

Emily shook her head. "Don't whine to me when
he pukes his guts out on your satin sheets.''

"Okay," Mary Lynn agreed sweetly. "But you
will come to the wedding, won't you?''

"I take it back," Emily said with a sigh. "You
guys aren't sick. You're pathetic.''

"But having fun," Jeannie argued. "Even you,
Miss Wouldn't Have Him on a China Plate, have to
admit this is pretty entertaining.''

Emily shifted in her chair so she could see Kurt,
who was keeping an eye on the beer bottles scattered
across the table in front of him. Once, sometime
around her sixteenth birthday, Emily had entertained
some very private and inappropriate fantasies about
Kurt herself. Looking back, she blamed a gawky
adolescence and an overstimulated imagination for
the six-week lapse in hostilities. Kurt had had a habit
of coming into the ice cream parlor where she

worked after school, and if she wasn't busy, he'd often as not stand around talking to her. But during those particular six weeks, he'd acted, well, *interested* in what she had to say, in the activities she talked about, the plans she was making for her future. They'd had actual *conversations,* and Emily had begun to think maybe she'd been wrong about Kurt all along. But then one day he'd brought Carolina with him. Carolina, who teased Emily about her cherry-vanilla crush on her older sister's boyfriend. Carolina, who staked her claim by kissing Kurt full on the lips in front of Emily, several customers and half a dozen passersby. Carolina, who managed to make what had seemed innocently exciting into something it wasn't. After that, Kurt didn't come for ice cream anymore—at least, not when Emily was there—and she'd buried her childish fantasies under a mountain of resentment. "I still say no woman in her right mind is going to spend actual money on the chance to win a drunken cowboy."

Genna reached for her wallet. "Who said anything about actual money? I'm using credit."

All across the tavern, women were riffling through their billfolds and waving dollar bills over their heads. Emily had to admit it was kind of fun to watch. Who would have thought so many women would be so eager to throw good money after a bad idea? "What do you guys think you're going to do if you win him?" she asked the four at her table.

"Take him home and keep him as a pet?" Renetta suggested.

Emily rolled her eyes. "You'll never get him housebroken."

Jeannie grinned. "I promise, Emily, if I'm the lucky cowgirl, I'll keep him on a short leash and out of your yard."

"If I win," Mary Lynn said with a sassy smile, "you can borrow him, Emily, because if there's any woman in this bar who needs a night of fantasy more than I do, it's you."

Genna tsked at that idea. "Emily, honey, the best thing for you to do is buy a bunch of tickets and give them to me. Because I swear on my Wonderbra that if I win that hunk of famous cowboy, I will not, under any circumstances, loan him to you."

"I'm not spending a dime on that man...even for fun." Emily lifted her glass of ginger ale. "It would be just my luck to win the son of a gopher."

"That'd be tragic." Jeannie signaled for another beer. "You'd wind up murdering him, and we'd wind up having to visit you every other Sunday over at the state correctional facility."

"Not to mention," Mary Lynn added, "it would be a sad waste of cowboy buns."

Scattered applause broke out like rain, and the women took over the lion's share of the noisemaking in their eagerness to take part in the raffle. Nellis and Sam had Kurt on his feet, leading him from table to table, and while they took orders for the raffle, he stood around, smiling a loopy smile. Since tickets were in short supply and beer wasn't, buying a beer for the center table equaled buying one chance in the raffle. Beer caps were used for tickets, and upon purchase, the cap was snapped off the bottle and handed to the purchaser along with a laundry marker. By the time all the caps were inscribed with a name and collected in a glass pitcher, even Emily was caught up in the laughter.

Soused or sober, Kurt was a force to contend with. His blue eyes sparkled with contagious amusement, his smile charmed the good sense right out of the womenfolk, and his slurred consonants only served to convince the crowd of the deep sincerity in his truly broken heart. When he and the escorts who were holding him upright finally stopped at their table, Emily had to stop herself from reaching into her pocketbook for the price of a beer. But the last thing she wanted was Carolina's former heartthrob, drunk as a sponge, depending on her for a ride home.

"Okay, we got it!" Sam announced in a voice slurred with excitement. "We're gonna raffle off ol' Kurtis, now. You women don't go holdin' your breath, 'cause it's gonna take us a minute or two to figure this out." He slid into his chair with boneless ease and hunkered over the table, consulting with Nellis and Max while they all drank another beer. Kurt stood beside the table, his ego—if not his dignity—held upright by the bevy of beauties crowding close. He bestowed his trademark smile on one and all and could have been fielding questions about where he bought his hats for all the notice he took of being first prize in a raffle. He didn't even seem to notice when a lanky blonde in a red leather skirt bopped her way to his side.

"Uh-oh," Genna said. "Look who's crashing the party."

"Is that Farrah?" Mary Lynn asked.

Emily craned her neck to get a better view, and her heart stuttered at the sight of Fortune City's femme fatale wriggling up to the man of the hour. "What has she done to her hair?"

"I'd call that color Heigh-ho Silver," Jeannie said. "I heard she was back from Reno with a fresh set of divorce papers and ready to sign up husband number four."

"That's not fair," Renetta said. "She's acting like she already won the raffle."

Sure enough, she had her hands on Kurt's chest and was moving her hips in a—well, Emily hadn't seen that move since high school, when Farrah had campaigned for homecoming queen one football player at a time. The years since hadn't given her any subtlety, either, and Emily had half a mind to march up and tell her to quit pawing Kurt like he was her very own rubbing post. "She probably believes Kurt will actually marry her if she wins."

Mary Lynn's chin sank into the cup of her hands. "It's beginning to look like *Kurt* believes he's going to marry her if she wins."

As if her words were a prophesy, Nellis Cohen and Sam Baxter rattled the beer caps in the pitcher. "Somebody give us a drum roll," Nellis said, and Kipp obediently drummed his fists on the table. "Okay, McCauley." Sam thrust the pitcher in front of Kurt, whose smile was three-quarters past coherence. "Stick yer hand in there and pick yerself a *woman!*"

Women cheered. Men whooped. Kurt stirred the beer caps and finally pulled out a winner.

"Who is it?" someone called from the back.

"Who's the lucky gal?" someone else yelled.

"Name your poison!" Steve Cutter slurred the *s* sound until he nearly passed out. "Tell us who she is!"

Kurt turned the winning bottle top in his palm, leaned his head in close to his hand, then drew back and squinted. "Can't read it," he mumbled.

"What'd you say?" a voice yelled out. "Who is she?"

Nellis braced his hands on the table and leaned across to look at the cap. "It's…it's… Hell, I cain't read it either."

"Here, allow me." Farrah had the cap in her hand before anyone quite knew she reached for it. She looked at it, and her eyes widened. "Oh, my," she said. "Oh, my. It's me. I win. I win!" She looked at Kurt with shining eyes. "Yes," she announced to his dumbfounded face. "Yes, I will marry you."

"Whoa," Mary Lynn said. "Is that a coincidence or what?"

"Coincidence, ha." Renetta crossed her skinny arms on the tabletop. "She cheated, pure and simple."

"Rotten, rotten, rotten," Genna declared. "The contest was rigged."

Emily sat in silence as Farrah kissed Kurt McCauley senseless…which wasn't saying much, since he'd been nearly senseless before she started. Still, the whole thing was decidedly unsettling. With a clear conscience, Emily could wish a mountain of bad luck on Kurt, but even she had to draw the line short of Farrah Phillips. Not that Kurt seemed all that bothered. Or any of the other men, for that matter. Truth be told, the men all seemed to think Kurt had just drawn a royal flush. They were singing "Goin' to the Chapel" with enhanced fervor and a few lyrics the song's composer had never heard.

"Now what?" Renetta asked. "He's not really going to marry her, is he?"

"Nah," Mary Lynn said, although her tone was a trifle uncertain. "Kurt couldn't be *that* drunk."

Emily thought he looked pretty happy, even for a guy with a beer in each hand and a blonde wrapped around his left side. "I guess this is as incredibly dumb as it's going to get tonight."

"One can only hope," Jeannie said, with no real conviction.

"He won't marry her." Genna drank the rest of her beer and pushed away from the table. "I say we all go home and find out tomorrow whether these idiots put him on a plane for Scottsdale or they so-bered up enough to just let him sleep off the rest of his misery."

Jeannie bent to retrieve her purse. "I'm with Gen. We came, we saw, we remembered why our mothers told us to stay away from those guys."

Emily knew she had to stop staring at the bizarre and risqué display going on center stage. She didn't care who Kurt McCauley kissed, who he slept with, or even who he married…as long as it wasn't her sister. *Or her.* Still, it was like a really bad made-for-television movie…she couldn't seem to find the wherewithal to turn it off.

"You staying, Em?" Mary Lynn asked.

"No," she said. "No, of course not."

They started for the door, but with a round of rowdy, discordant laughter, Kurt's friends reclaimed the whole room's attention. "We need a volunteer," Sam called to near and far. "We need a desig—desig—a designated driver to transport this here weddin' party to Vegas. Anybody, besides Otis, who ain't been drinkin?''

Apparently, everyone in the bar had been planning on either walking home or calling for Fortune City's only taxicab, because no one claimed to be in any shape to drive. "She didn't drink," the snippy little waitress said into the sudden lack of response. "Her."

Emily realized with a sick feeling that an index finger and practically every eye in the joint were turned in her direction.

"Her," the waitress said again. "That girl."

"Emily Dawson," Jeannie said loudly, in case anyone might have missed the finger of accusation. "That's right, Emily. You only drank ginger ale."

"Hey, and she drives that big van, too." Kipp grinned, obviously pleased that he knew that tidbit of information. "Cool! We can *all* go to witness the weddin'."

"I'm not—" Emily began, but her protest was lost in a wave of enthusiasm and she was caught up in a surge of friends, acquaintances and the fervor of a sudden wild rush to the door, the chapel...or possibly Nova Scotia.

## Chapter Two

Emily had miscalculated from the start. In hindsight, it was easy to see that she should never have gone to the Silver Dollar Cowboy Saloon in the first place. Certainly, she should never have let five no-account cowboys commandeer her van...and her services as chauffeur. She was sober and they weren't, went their argument. Her van was big enough for all of them, they said. It was, they pointed out, just a thirty-minute trip into Las Vegas, thirty minutes back, fun for all and all for fun...and if she didn't drive them, they'd just find somebody else to do it, and she'd wind up missing the wedding of the century because of some silly principle.

She should have called their bluff, kept her keys in her purse and her purse closed. She should have stood her ground on the principle—silly or not—that they were drunk as skunks and had no idea what was mischief and what wasn't. She definitely shouldn't have started out with them all packed into her big van like so many pickled herring...even if her original intention had been to simply deliver each of them—grumpy perhaps, but safely—to their respective houses.

Once they arrived in Las Vegas, it was a no-brainer to realize she should have dropped the whole vanload in the middle of nowhere and let the long walk home sober them up. But everyone seemed to be having a great time. Certainly her old commercial van had rarely, if ever, contained such a merry crew. Even Jeannie and Genna, who had refused to be left behind, saw no harm in cheering on the raffle winner and her prize catch. So why was Emily the only one who fretted about it? After all, Kurt might be an idiot, but he wasn't a fool. He'd never marry Farrah...no matter what condition he was in or how much encouragement he got. Would he?

"I haven't had this much fun since the inmate rodeo came to town." Genna giggled as she leaned forward between the two front seats. "I wish Mary Lynn and Renetta had come with us."

"Somebody had to make sure Cooper got home. He was nearly comatose," Jeannie stated bluntly from the passenger seat, where she was riding shotgun. "Besides, Renetta's too young and impressionable to appreciate the fine art of dumbness being practiced here tonight."

"Ten bucks!" someone in the back yelled. "I got

ten bucks says Kipp can belch the whole entire song of 'Jingle Bells.'"

"You're right," Emily said. "It takes a high level of maturity to be able to appreciate something like that."

Genna laughed. "I can't wait to hear what Carolina will have to say about this little road trip."

Emily wasn't eager to tell anyone about her part in this incredibly dumb stunt, least of all her sister. It would be just like Carolina to profess shock and dismay while gloating for the rest of her life that poor Kurt had been so desperate with love for her he'd raffled himself into a loveless marriage to prove he could never love another...and she would never, ever allow Emily to forget her part in aiding and abetting him. Not that Emily was apt to forget it anytime soon, anyway. The thought of Kurt saying "I do" to Farrah Phillips made her stomach churn. "You don't think Farrah actually believes he's going to marry her, do you?"

"Sure, she does," Jeannie said with conviction. "That girl's in it for keeps. Or at least as long as it takes to get community property."

"Uh-oh. Community property." Genna's voice was filled with sudden concern. "I hadn't thought about that angle."

Jeannie shrugged. "You can bet dollars to doughnuts that Farrah has. Remember how she was in high school? She wanted the trophies. All of them. Cheerleading. Basketball. Boyfriends. And she didn't have many scruples about how she got them, either.''

"No scruples at all, as I remember," Genna said with a frown. "This could be bad."

Jeannie gave a sage nod. "Farrah's been working her way up the food chain for three husbands now. Kurt's next in line on her investment portfolio."

"Kurt isn't dumb enough to marry her," Emily stated firmly. "Not that I think he's all that smart, you understand, but he knows what she's like."

Genna tossed a glance toward the back of the van. "I'm only guessing, but I'd say tonight her character isn't uppermost in his mind."

"She's got him primed, all right," Jeannie said.

Emily felt sick. "I shouldn't have driven them over here."

"Someone else would have, Em. You might as well relax and enjoy the show. It's not like Kurt McCauley is your responsibility."

"Yeah," Genna agreed. "It's not as if anyone expects you to save him from being a dumb ass."

"As if you had a snowball's chance of doing that, anyway." Jeannie glanced toward the back of the van, where Kipp was belching, Nellis and Sam were laughing, Max was telling a tall tale to no one in particular, and Farrah was hovering over Kurt like a black widow spider. "Farrah has her raffle ticket to matrimony firmly in hand."

Obviously aware of their pointed scrutiny, Farrah

tore her attention from Kurt long enough to call out, "Don't miss your turn, Emily. The courthouse is in the next block."

Sure enough, Emily saw a sign on the left indicating that the Clark County Courthouse—where marriage licenses could be obtained from morning to midnight through the week and twenty-four hours a day on the weekends—was dead ahead. "She's going to get a license," Emily said, the knot of anxiety clenching taut inside her.

Genna sighed dramatically. "She must know the wedding chapel routine by heart. How are we going to stop her?"

"We?" Emily asked with a gulp. "You just said he wasn't our responsibility."

"I said he wasn't your responsibility, Em. Jeannie and I, on the other hand, have a moral obligation to single women everywhere to keep him out of Farrah's greedy little clutches."

"True," Jeannie concurred. "Farrah's already had two more husbands than I have and three more than the two of you. She has to be stopped before she can besmirch yet another innocent bachelor."

"*Besmirch?*" As Emily made the turn, she glanced in the rearview mirror at the poor innocent, who seemed blissfully unaware of being *smirched*. Perhaps because he was so busy being *smooched*. "Do the single women of the world a favor and let her have him."

"Oh, come on, Emily," Genna said. "Even you must feel a few qualms about just turning him over to someone like *her*. Whether you want to admit it or not, he's basically a nice guy."

Oh, sure, Emily thought. Kurt was such a nice guy that he'd made her life miserable, treating her like a pesky mosquito whenever he came courting Carolina. And if he was so nice, why had he turned down her business proposition without even the courtesy of a personal refusal? After he'd been the voice of encouragement all those years ago, when she'd first confided her plans to open a clothing store. But, *no*, he'd told her intermediary. *No*, the intermediary had relayed to her. *No*, she said to any claims Kurt McCauley might make to being a nice guy. "I think Farrah deserves him," Emily said flatly, despite the truth—that she didn't like seeing Kurt with Farrah. Of course, she'd never liked seeing Kurt with Carolina, either.

"Not me." Jeannie rummaged through her knapsack of a purse. "Nice guy or not, no man deserves to wake up and find himself with a hangover *and* a sea hag of a wife. There…" She pulled out a small black cylinder and held it up proudly. "Defense spray," she said. "This'll stop that buffalo gal in her diabolical tracks. But you guys will have to help, because I'm not wasting the whole bottle on her."

"Put that away." Emily rolled the van to a reluctant stop in front of the courthouse and turned off the engine. "If Farrah means to marry Kurt and he's not sober or smart enough to stop her, then we definitely aren't jumping in the middle of it. Understand?"

"Sure." Jeannie dropped the bottle into her pocket. "I'm just going to take it along in case Kurt decides he wants to marry me."

"You'd spray him?" Genna wanted to know.

"Shoot, no." Jeannie said with a grin. "I'm sprayin' anybody who tries to stop him."

It was no fun being sober in this crowd, Emily decided as she got out of the van and went around to open the sliding side door, which had long since stopped working from the inside. Someone—several someones, by the sound of it—were already pounding on the door, and for a moment Emily thought about just leaving them in there for the duration of the night. But then, she was the designated driver, not the baby-sitter.

The door stuck, as usual, and Emily had to give it a sound thump with the flat of her hand before it rolled out of the way. Then she reluctantly stepped aside. No good reason for her to stand in the path of true love.

KURT WAS HAVING an out-of-body experience. Or maybe it was one of those out-of-sight, out-of-mind episodes. Either way, he was having trouble keeping track of who was out of sight, who was out of mind and just where in hell he was. There wasn't much doubt that he'd had too much to drink because there were about a thousand echoes inside his head and a thousand more in this sardine can he was riding in. Everyone was laughing, him included, which had to be a good sign. His friends kept slapping him on the back, too, and someone who smelled like incense was kissing him...which was usually a sign that more good times lay ahead.

He was getting married, the echoes told him, and Kurt thought that was funny because he'd had some nutty dream that Carolina had married somebody else. Which was crazy, because she knew he meant to marry her. She had to be waiting for him at the church, he supposed, because he was pretty sure she wasn't the one who kept kissing him. That, he figured, had to be one of the bridesmaids.

When the van stopped, he was ready. He should have married Carolina years ago and put them both out of their misery. But it wasn't too late. *Get the license,* someone was saying, and through a fog of bleary thoughts, Kurt saw the side door of the van open, and there she was. Carolina. Her hair turned to burnt sienna in the moonlight. Or maybe it was a streetlight. But he'd recognize that mouth anywhere. And those eyes. Blue, he thought. Or maybe brown. He flat couldn't remember. Hell, he hadn't seen her in nearly two years. A man couldn't be expected to remember every little detail about the woman he loved. Well, tonight he'd just marry her, and then he could look at her eyes and see what color they were any time he felt like it. "Carolina," he said, feeling his smile slide all over his face. "We're gettin' married." Then he pulled her into his arms and kissed her soundly, just to prove he finally meant it.

EMILY should have put her foot down there and then, hard, on Kurt's big foot. If he hadn't taken her by surprise, she was sure she would have stomped him, sure she would have informed him that he had drunkenly mistaken her for her sister and that she, Emily, wouldn't marry him if he were the last cowboy on earth. In the world. In the whole dang universe. And she didn't appreciate him kissing her, either.

Yes, she would definitely have told him…except that his lips were firmer than she'd thought they could be. And the mustache she despised wasn't the wiry distraction she'd always imagined it would be…if she'd ever imagined being this close to it, which she definitely hadn't. Well, not since she was sixteen, anyway, and he hadn't even had a mustache then. Still, for a man who had to be defying several laws of brain cell chemistry by managing to stand on his own two feet, he was a darn good kisser. And for a woman who was defying her own rock-hard resolutions to keep a minimum distance of a hundred miles between her person and his, she was giving a darn good impression of an idiot.

"Hey! Wait a minute!" Farrah's outraged voice sounded like it came from a block away, but apparently she was much closer, because Kurt's lips were abruptly pulled from Emily's with ferocious haste. "I won him, fair and square," Farrah said at the top of her considerable lungs. "And no little Goody Two-shoes Dawson is going to get her mitts on him. I'm the one he's going to marry. Now. Tonight. So let go of him."

Emily realized with a start that her arms were wrapped around Kurt's neck, and she surprised herself by keeping them there. "He doesn't want to marry you, Farrah," she heard herself saying. "Not now. Not tonight. Not ever. So *you* let go."

Jeannie and Genna came up on either side of Emily, facing the blonde and Kurt, who wore a sloppy, disoriented grin. "You tell her, Em," Genna said. "Don't let that peroxide petunia take your man."

"*Her* man?" Farrah nearly strangled on the words. "Like hell he's hers!"

"She's standing in for Carolina," Jeannie said. "So back off, Bozette!"

Emily felt vindicated, as if maybe it *was* her responsibility to save Kurt from Farrah's lethal clutches, as if kissing him was somehow her duty as a red-blooded American woman. "Yeah," she said, echoing Jeannie's stand-and-deliver tone. "Just back off."

Farrah's mouth tightened into an unattractive frown, and she took a menacing step forward. Emily began to rethink her rescue mission. The men tumbled out of the van, suddenly aware of the entertainment potential.

"What's this?" Max drawled. "A catfight?"

"A catfight?" Kipp Trowbridge jumped from the van and klutzily caught his balance. "Who's fightin'?"

"Women!" Nellis clapped his hands in what would have been enthusiastic applause if he could have managed to connect one palm with the other. "Give 'em room! The *women* are gonna brawl!"

Sam cupped his hands to his mouth, as if he wasn't sure his voice would carry. "I got ten bucks says Emily can take her!"

Confused, Emily frowned at the boisterous group surrounding her. Farrah kept pulling at her arms, the men were rooting for a "hair-pullin', eye-scratchin' fight," Jeannie and Genna were noisily offering their opinions and advice, Kurt kept smiling that loopy smile at her…and before she could gather her thoughts and decide how to get the whole bunch inside the van, he bent his head and kissed her again. Not quite so awkwardly this time. With a bit more finesse and a whole lot more purpose. With enough energy and sheer skill that her knees wobbled like jelly. Despite being sober, sensible and sane, Emily kissed him back, thinking that maybe he didn't deserve to have to marry Farrah, no matter what his past sins might have been.

"We're gettin' married, Carolina," he stated in a voice of finality, slurring just a little over the name. "Tonight."

"That is *not* Carolina," Farrah protested, loud and strong. "It's only her sister."

Kurt narrowed bloodshot eyes on Emily. "Close enough," he said, and taking her hand, he pulled her toward the courthouse.

"No," EMILY SAID firmly. "No way. No how. No. I am not going to marry him."

"You signed for the license." Jeannie picked up a bouquet of artificial flowers from a table in the foyer of the Lovebird Lane Wedding Chapel and thrust it into Emily's hand. "And it's not like you can't get the whole thing annulled tomorrow."

"Tomorrow?" Emily repeated as if that actually made sense.

"Well, the day after, maybe, but it wouldn't be complicated to do, you know."

Complicated? Oh, no, getting an annulment wouldn't be complicated at all, because she wasn't going through with this stupid ceremony in the first place. There had been a moment at the license counter when everyone had been talking at once and she'd been explaining to Kurt, who was past listening, that she had no intention of applying for a marriage license with him or anyone else, when he'd touched her cheek with the back of his fingers, when he'd smiled gently, albeit drunkenly, and said, "Sign." And she had. Just like that. Stupidly, like a woman who will believe anything is possible when it comes to long kisses under a romantic moon. Or streetlight. But she'd since come to her senses. "I'm not doing this," Emily warned. "I signed for the license because I thought that would put an end to it. I thought Farrah would shut up and the guys would pass out and we'd all go home and—"

"—and Kurt would frame the marriage license and hang it on his wall to remind him of the day you saved his unworthy butt." Jeannie stepped back to observe the bouquet, then took it and replaced it with a single yellow paper rose tied with an ornate and flowing white ribbon. "He's not going to be appreciative, Em. He's probably not even going to remember any of this tomorrow morning. But the idiots here with him—and that includes Gold Digger Phillips—aren't drunk enough to pass out, even though they are too inebriated to let any of us go home until there's some kind of ceremony. Now, nobody twisted your arm to walk into that courthouse and sign up for a marriage license, so now you're stuck in the role of blushing bride. I, for one, think you need to finish what you started."

Genna took Emily's elbow and pulled her toward the arched doorway, past a wall of posters advertising everything from honeymoon specials to a radio station's win-a-classic contest. "Think of it as doing your bit for women who go nuts over Wrangler butts."

Emily wished she'd had the foresight to tie two-ton weights to her feet. "I fail to see how my being incredibly stupid could benefit anyone, least of all women who measure a man by the seat of his pants."

Nellis pushed aside the lovebird-blue curtain that draped the chapel entrance and frowned at the three women. "What's the holdup?" he asked. "I'm not sure how much longer Kipp and Max can keep Farrah outside. She's puttin' up one hullabaloo of a fight. Plus, Kurt's gettin' impatient, says he shoulda got married years ago."

Emily dug in her heels. "He thinks he's marrying Carolina."

"He's drunk, Emily," Jeannie pointed out unnecessarily. "And he's bound and determined to marry somebody before he leaves here. If you bow out, Farrah will bow right in. He could think he was marryin' Madonna, for all the difference it would make to her."

Genna raised an eyebrow. "Jeannie's right, Em. Nobody twisted your arm to step in and take Farrah's place, but it's done. Now, march down that aisle and let the preacher say the words that'll put Farrah out of her misery and save Kurt from gettin' into a marriage he can't easily get out of.''

Refusal was on the tip of her tongue, denial pushing right behind it. But then Emily looked up and saw Kurt at the front of the heavenly blue chapel, and the words formed a knot in her throat. This was crazy. Nuts. Completely insane. She did not want to marry anyone, least of all him. She didn't want to save him from the consequences of his own stupid actions. It wasn't her fault he'd tried to mend his supposedly broken heart with one too many beers. It wasn't her fault Carolina had gotten tired of waiting for him to save her from spinsterhood. It definitely wasn't her fault that he wasn't smart enough to realize getting married was the last thing he ought to be doing at the moment. She couldn't think of a single good reason that she should be the one to save Kurt. She could, in fact, think of several solid reasons not to. But when he looked up and saw her, his rugged features went soft with pleasure, his blue eyes smiled with pure delight, and somehow—as incredibly dumb as it was—she was sixteen again and he was smiling at *her*, talking to *her*, wanting *her*. There and then, for better or worse, she knew she couldn't let Farrah Phillips take him home as a trophy.

"I'm going to regret this," she said, cupping the fake rose in both hands as she turned toward the doorway. "No, I take that back. I *already* regret this."

"Don't worry." Jeannie patted Emily's back with either consolation or encouragement. Maybe both. "You're not going to regret it half as much as he will."

Which was true enough, Emily admitted as she walked down the narrow aisle to a tinny version of *Lohengrin*. At the end of the rows of white-draped chairs, Nellis supported Kurt with a silly grin and a reinforcing arm. Both men listed slightly to one side, but when Kurt smiled at her approach, her feather-brained heart raced like a kid at recess. He was too drunk to know what he was doing with whom. He thought she was Carolina, for Pete's sake, and when he found out she wasn't…well, he was going to be plenty mad. Which, now that she thought about it, was the best reason of all for Emily to finish what she'd so foolishly started. No matter how inane and incredible her behavior, Kurt was going to feel worse. And that thought alone made her feel better. Not much. But some.

If only he hadn't kissed her…

"Emily Georgia Dawson," the minister intoned. "Will you take this man…?"

# Chapter Three

Some days it just didn't pay to get out of bed. Or into it.

Emily stopped pacing to look at the bed she'd gotten herself into. It was roomy enough for four, but there was only one lump beneath the covers. One big, dumb lump. Sighing, she started pacing again. Five comfortable steps to the window. Five uncomfortable steps back to the bed. Why had she done something so *stupid?* Driving the van was one thing. Marrying Kurt McCauley to save him from Farrah Phillips was quite another. She couldn't even complain that she'd been drunk and therefore unaccountable for her actions. Oh, no. She had no excuse. None. Zero. Zilch. A schoolgirl's fantasy had stuck her smack between reason and rationalizing and landed her square in the middle of this mess. When Kurt woke up—which he was bound to do sooner or later—he was going to murder her. Unless she got him first. Honeymoon in Vegas Results in

Double Homicide, the newspapers would read…and her name would be forever linked with the one cowboy she wished she'd never met.

Stupid, she thought as she paced some more. Stupid, stupid, stupid. It would have been better to let Farrah have him and let Kurt deal with the consequences of being the booby prize in a cowboy raffle. But sometime after he'd kissed her—twice—somewhere in the midst of Farrah's escalating demands and her friends' assurances that she could easily say I do tonight and annul the marriage tomorrow, she'd lost sight of the fact that Kurt McCauley was not her responsibility. Somehow she'd forgotten that she didn't even like him, much less care who he did or didn't marry.

Well, now she cared. Now she really cared.

Stopping at the window of the hotel room, she looked out at the night lights of Las Vegas and wondered where her friends were now. Probably halfway home in the rented limo they'd somehow wrangled out of the wedding chapel. She already knew how their defense would go. *We had to get Farrah away from you and Kurt.* That would be their argument. *She was set on pulling your hair out by the roots or getting us all arrested,* they'd say. *Somebody had to make sure she didn't slip back and murder the two of you,* they'd point out. *By the time the annulment comes through, she'll be on to new prospects,* they'd add for good measure. All of which might be true.

But to a man—Genna and Jeannie included—they'd deserted Emily, leaving her to deal with the aftermath of that ill-advised five-minute ceremony. Well, someone was going to pay for this incredibly dumb stunt, and it wasn't going to be her.

She'd meant to give Kurt a scathing piece of her mind the minute they were alone in the hotel room and then hightail it home. But, oblivious to her intentions, he'd taken one look at the bed, stripped down to pin-striped boxers and a single sock and crawled under the covers, leaving her with not only the piece of mind she'd meant to give him, but the awful realization that he wasn't going to be awake to hear her demand for an immediate annulment for a good long while.

She ought to leave him where he lay, retrieve her van from its parking space and head for home. Let him find out what an incredibly stupid thing he'd done when the sheriff served him with annulment papers. But that would mean she'd have to live with the incredibly stupid thing *she'd* done longer than was absolutely necessary...which was one second too long. Better to stay in the hotel room Nellis and Max had insisted the newlyweds should have, and get this all out in the open as soon as Kurt was coherent. The thought of hitting him with both barrels provided some comfort. She imagined the moment, sometime tomorrow, when he would peel back the eyelids of his infamous bedroom blue eyes and begin to suffer the pains of a well-deserved hangover. Then, just as he came to terms with the horrific headache and realized he wasn't going to die, she'd inform him that not only was he married, he was married to *her*. True, it wasn't the kind of pain Emily would have liked to inflict as payback for all the times he'd alternately ignored and irritated her, but it would do for starters.

In the meantime, she might as well get some sleep. She wanted to be at her best tomorrow, if only because it would put Kurt at a further disadvantage. Not that she expected to come out of this smelling like a rose, but adding lack of sleep to her list of bad choices wasn't going to help, either. Eyeing the bed and Kurt, who had barely moved since he'd fallen into it, she decided there was room for a hockey team. Besides, what difference did it make if they shared a bed for this, the only night of their ill-fated marriage? It wasn't as if anyone in Fortune City would believe sleep was all they'd shared. There would be jokes and sly remarks from the Silver Dollar to the Baptist church. No one would believe wild man Kurt McCauley had fallen into bed without so much as a glance at her. No one with the possible exception of Jeannie, Genna, Mary Lynn and Renetta would ever believe Emily could have passed up the chance to have sex with the handsome hunk of cowboy currently sleeping in her bed.

He stirred in his sleep and softly snored.

*Disgusting.* Emily pulled back the covers and slipped into bed as far from him and as close to the edge as possible. *Downright disgusting.*

KURT KNEW he wasn't alone. From the hazy cocoon of a deep and dreamless sleep, he reached out to pet Melba and scoot her onto her side of the bed. But the warm shape beneath his palm was not the small body of his Jack Russell terrier. It was longer, larger, wore cotton, had curves. Hmm, he thought, cupping a nicely rounded breast. This was a definite improvement in bed buddies. A breath of a memory skimmed his thoughts and drifted away. He let it go. He'd never been one to quarrel with fate. *Lucky stiff,* he congratulated himself, and went back to sleep.

EMILY snuggled down, cuddling against the toasty warmth at her back. She sensed the light in the room was morning sun but refused to open her eyes and confirm it. She hadn't slept so well in ages. Maybe that old devil sandman had brought her a new mattress while she slept. Lord knew she needed one. Maybe she was in the midst of a pleasant dream where the earth was made of pillow tops and sleep was the worldwide currency.

*Snarf.*

The sound behind her and the puff of warm breath on her neck came at the same instant, and made her stiffen from the roots of her hair all the way to the tips of her ruby-painted toenails. Her eyes flew open, and she stayed perfectly still—and as memory returned, perfectly horrified.

She was in bed with Kurt McCauley. Not just in the same bed, either. Oh, no, she was spooned against him like leftover tapioca stuck to the sides of the bowl. His arm was draped over hers as if he was accustomed to sleeping beside her. Yeah, right. He was accustomed to sleeping beside a woman, maybe, but not her. Definitely not her. She held her breath and slid one foot toward the edge of the mattress, which suddenly seemed to stretch the width of a football field. His breathing changed, his soft snore dropped into a sigh, and his arm pulled her against him, his hand tucked just below her breast, his fingers cradling the under slope.

*Sheesh,* Emily thought. Even asleep, the man couldn't keep his hands to himself. Before she'd gotten old enough to have boyfriends of her own, she used to spy on her sister. There were lots of boys back then, but Kurt was the only one worth watching. There was lots of kissing when he was around. Lots of other stuff, too. Stuff that Emily couldn't get close enough to see, but she could tell from the way Carolina dimpled when she pushed his hands away that Kurt was her sister's favorite. And she could tell by the way Kurt laughed that he knew it. Spying on them had been her introduction to the courtship rituals between males and females, the basis for her opinion that most men were drooling fools in the hands of a beautiful woman.

Probably that was the reason Emily rarely had more than three dates with the same man. Sometime after the second date but before the fourth, she made a point of showing Carolina's picture, and if there was so much as a flash of interest in her date's expression, she knew there was no point in taking the relationship any further. She was taking no chances on falling for a guy who ever had been or might in the future be in love with Carolina. It wasn't fair, she knew. There had probably been some decent men this culling process had given short shrift. But she'd spent enough time in her sister's shadow. Definitely, she'd spent enough time watching Carolina charm the socks off the men of Culver County. And Kurt had lost more socks than most.

And now Emily Dawson was married to him.

Carolina would never forgive her.

Which was a lot sooner than Emily was likely to forgive herself.

Uncaring if she woke him, she scrambled from under the covers and hit the floor running. Well, not running, exactly, but she wanted distance between them, as fast as possible. And perspective—she wanted that, too. Might as well add an annulment to the list of things she wanted. An annulment as quick and painless as the wedding that was forever—or at least until Emily burned it—memorialized in the five-by-seven photo on the dresser.

But she figured getting out of this marriage wouldn't be quick or easy. For one thing, there was no love lost between her and Kurt—which *should* make everything simpler, but wouldn't. For another, by midafternoon, there wouldn't be a solitary soul in Fortune City who hadn't heard about the cowboy raffle, the quickie Las Vegas wedding and the bride swap in the final crucial moments. Emily shoved a shaky hand through her mop of unruly hair and figured she'd be lucky to survive with her sense of humor intact. She'd be lucky if Farrah Phillips didn't sue her for alienation of affection or Grand Theft Raffle Ticket.

*Snarf.* Kurt's snoring grew rhythmic and controlled, a not wholly unpleasant sound to remind her that every time she got near him, she wound up thinking of ways to permanently wipe his annoying smile right off his annoying face. This morning, she figured she had the best shot she was ever likely to get.

KURT BLINKED, yawned and rolled onto his back. A dull ache all over his body mirrored a steady throbbing inside his head. It had been a long time since his last hangover, but he recognized the symptoms—right down to waking up with the mother of all headaches. He'd given up juvenile machismo a long time ago, had figured out early that excessive drinking wasn't good for mind, body or spirit. So how in hell had he let Nellis and the rest of the wild bunch talk him into going to the Silver Dollar? Oh, sure, at the time, he'd thought—and said—that his heart was broken, but that was no excuse. He knew better than to head for the saloon, had known for years that the old gang fell into old habits whenever they got together. Getting drunk had been the measure of manhood in high school, and Kurt wondered sometimes if drinking was all they had left in common.

Something clattered on the other side of a wall, and Kurt winced, vowing silently never to touch another beer for as long as he lived. Or at least until his head stopped its incessant pounding. Turning his head carefully on the pillow, he checked his surroundings. It didn't take much to know he wasn't in his own bed. The sheets were wildly rumpled, so he'd either had a rough night or he had more to worry about than a nasty hangover. He had a hazy memory of long, wet kisses and a breast that nicely fit the cup of his hand, but little more. He wrestled with the headache as he pushed onto his elbows and squinted at the light pouring in from the window. Cupping one hand to shade his eyes, Kurt tried to remember details of how he'd come to be in an unfamiliar bed in a strange hotel room.

Somewhere, a shower was running. Beyond the

blinding brightness of the sun coming through the open drapes, he could see that the bathroom door was closed. With a groan, he leaned back and laid his arm across his eyes. *Okay, McCauley. The shades are open, the sunlight's pouring in, and someone's in the shower.* The last time he'd passed out and awakened in a strange hotel room, he'd been a heck of a lot younger and remembered a hell of a lot more about the night before. He frowned, trying to recall any detail from the vast black hole that seemed to be his memory.

Nothing…except the kisses and the breast.

He sat up to gather clues. Daytime, definitely. Hotel room, who knew where. Head indentation on the pillow beside him. His clothes, dropped where they'd come off, in random clumps leading from the front door to the bed. Shirt. Boots. Belt. Jeans. Hell, he must have been in heat. With a groan, he leaned over and checked the carpet next to the bed. Sock. Just one. He didn't even want to know where the other was.

There was no sign of her clothes, although there was a purse on the dresser and a pair of brown Dexters on the floor. Things were looking pretty cozy all around. It was circumstantial evidence, sure. But if she was still here and felt cheery enough to open the damn drapes, something must have happened…and it must not have been too bad.

Rubbing the back of his neck, Kurt frowned,

scratched his chest and hoped she wasn't a complete stranger. On the other hand, he hoped she wasn't anyone he knew very well, either. Otherwise…well, he didn't want to think about otherwise. Women were so touchy about sex. Having it. Not having it. What happened before, during and after. This day and age, it was hard for a man to know how to act. The before part, well, that wasn't so hard. And during…he personally had never had any trouble there. But after…well, there was the burr in the saddle blanket.

With a sigh, he decided he'd just as soon find out now if he was going to get out of this with some aspirin and a few smiles or if the price was going to be a bit steeper. Breakfast, maybe. Or lunch, if it was past noon. He didn't want her to think he was a complete jerk. But supper? No, definitely, he was long gone by supper, no matter who she turned out to be. He got up, rubbed his forehead, pushed a hand through his hair and headed for the shower.

EMILY was feeling better. The hot water rained over her in calming cascades, and the simple act of shampooing made her feel like she was washing last night's fiasco right out of her hair. If only it could be that easy. Still, she wanted her wits about her when Kurt woke up. Not that he'd shown a sign of life, other than snoring, since he'd fallen dead drunk into the bed. Maybe she'd have some breakfast before she roused him. After all, this little honeymoon was on his charge card, and what was he going to say? Thanks for saving me from Farrah, but I'm not paying for your breakfast?

Of course, he wasn't apt to see her rescue as *saving* him. He wasn't apt to see that he'd been in the slightest danger. In truth, he wasn't apt to thank her for anything she'd done the night before. On the other hand, she didn't expect any thanks. It might ruin her low opinion of the man.

Emily ducked her head under the spray and let the water beat down on her illusions. Okay, so she didn't dislike him as much as she let on. And, in weaker moments, she could admit that he looked damn good in a pair of Wranglers. She'd even seen him behave with perfect charm, if not perfect manners. But that didn't change the fact that he was still in love with her sister and that, at the crucial moment, he'd believed he *was* marrying Carolina. Emily shook her head vigorously, and her wet hair slapped her on the back. There were days, she thought, when a person really shouldn't get out of bed.

The shower curtain puffed inward then out with a sudden draft, a deep voice boomed, "Scoot over, darlin'!" and the next thing Emily knew, the curtain was jerked aside and she was face to face—and nude to nude—with a tousled, blue-eyed, and big-grinning cowboy.

His grin didn't fade—it made a suicide leap off his lips. She didn't scream—she gulped in surprise, and her hands flew to the fig-leaf positions. His hands reflexively crossed over his private parts. And there they stood, staring at each other, caught in a shower of disaster.

KURT had shed his underwear just outside the bathroom door, thinking it would be easier to pretend he knew who was in the shower if he was in the process of getting in with her. Dumb move, he thought. Really dumb. Because, unless he was having one bizarre nightmare, the woman facing him was Carolina's kid sister. "Emily?" he said in a voice that squeaked. "Emily Dawson?"

A tentative nod confirmed his fears. The slight lift of one small shoulder sent a knot of self-disgust clenching in his gut. So much for the hope that he'd be out of this by noon.

"G-good morning," she said, swallowing hard. "I, uh, was just thinking about having breakfast."

She punctuated the statement with a wince, as if she didn't know what else to say. Which he could completely understand. This was a damned awkward moment. Taking a step back, he offered her the shower curtain and was ashamed of himself for not having the moral fortitude to resist admiring her body in the few seconds before she grabbed the vinyl liner and pulled it closed with a jerk. Kurt glanced at himself in the mirror, but saw only a vaguely dumbfounded expression in the fog that covered his reflection. Or maybe his vision was still fuzzy from all the beer in his system. Certainly his brain was still in a pea soup—because all he could think about was how bad his head hurt and how much he wanted to yank open that curtain and get a better look at the alluring shape behind it. A shape, he reminded the man on the other side of the haze, that belonged to Emily Dawson. Into the bongo-drum beat inside his head dropped a fragment of memory, the one involving his hand cupped around a breast. And he suddenly felt worse. A lot worse.

"Uh, Emily," he said cautiously, hoping somewhere deep in his soul that he hadn't…that she didn't…that there was another explanation for her being in this particular shower on this particular morning after. "Did I…did you…did we…?"

The curtain curled into a lazy S, revealing only her face in the opening. Steam swirled around her slicked-back hair in a soft, white halo, but there was a spark of hell fire in her deep brown eyes. "Yes," she said tightly. "We did."

Just as the knot in his stomach replicated itself in his throat and he silently and fervently repeated his vow to never, *ever* touch liquor again for the rest of his life, her voice softened to a croon. "Don't you remember?"

Trapped. No matter what answer he made to that

question, he was in bull hokey all the way up to his red neck. "Uh, sure," he said, reaching for the doorknob. "Are you kidding? Like I could forget last night." His short laugh was as forced as it felt. "I'll, uh, order breakfast." Then he was out the door and pulling on his boxers faster than a quarter horse could jump-start a race. Emily, he thought. He'd spent the night with Emily Dawson.

The images that brought to mind weren't nearly as appalling as he wanted them to be. Just the opposite, in fact, and if he recollected last night's kisses right, there was a whale of a lot more passion in Emily than he'd ever suspected. He only wished he could remember more about experiencing it. Still, he had no business being here with her. Sleeping with Carolina's sister was not an acceptable way of soothing a broken heart. At the moment, it was even hard to tell if his heart *was* broken, considering all his other aches and pains. Not the least of which was a major league regret.

*Emily.* Jeez, he *was* a jerk.

The guilt sent his hand raking through his hair, but one glance at her purse stilled it at the back of his head. Slowly, careful not to move any faster than absolutely necessary, he reached for the photograph laying crookedly half under the purse. His head throbbed with hangover, his whole body ached with a good imitation of having been thrown by a tough bronc, his brain was reeling with the discovery that he'd just had sex with the one woman he shouldn't even share the same county with, but there was nothing wrong with his eyesight. He was there in the photo, grinning like a loon, looking like a man who had the world by its Coronas. The fact that he was obviously in a wedding chapel registered a mild three point six on the Richter scale, but the fact that Emily was standing beside him, looking bridal, sent his equilibrium spinning clear off the charts.

EMILY turned up the cold water and deliberately stepped under the spray. "You're a nincompoop," she said aloud. "Why couldn't you just have told him straight out, 'Kurt McCauley, you're an idiot and I want an annulment of this ridiculous marriage.'"

Maybe because she hadn't realized how broad he was across the chest. Hadn't known his arms were so nicely muscled. Hadn't a clue that his body would taper the way it did…or *where* it did. Hadn't known the sight of a man's—well, the part he usually kept under wraps—could knock the breath right out of her lungs. She gave the tap another twist toward freezing and forced herself to stand under it, attempting to cool off her racing heartbeat, if not her racing thoughts. He'd nearly scared her to death, pulling back the shower curtain as he had. Her first thought had been that she'd married a psycho and they'd never find her body. Her second thought, no more coherent than the first, was that he had definite tan lines. Her third was scalding embarrassment that he was seeing her naked, which resulted in her limp parroting of some idea about ordering breakfast. But her fourth thought registered his words— "Scoot over, darlin'"—and after that, she was consumed with wanting to punch his arrogant lights out.

*Scoot over, darlin'?* He woke up from a dead sleep in a strange hotel room, walked into the bathroom without knocking and just got into the shower with whoever happened to be in there? What kind of pervert was he? And why hadn't she seized the opportunity to yank him by the part he usually kept under wraps into the shower and drown him?

Because that would be too good for him, that's why. He deserved to suffer. She didn't know how— she wasn't exactly sure why—but she knew it was her responsibility to the women who "go nuts over Wrangler butts" to take this maverick down a few notches. It was her duty as a smart, savvy female who needed a man in her life about as much as she needed another piece of Tupperware. Emily's teeth started to chatter, but she stayed an extra few seconds under the cold spray, hoping somehow she'd begin to understand how a smart, savvy female like her had wound up married to such a big, dumb lump of a cowboy.

PHOTO IN HAND, Kurt jerked open the bathroom door, forgetting that he'd meant to be fully dressed before he faced her again. "What kind of sick joke is this?" he asked, struggling to keep hysteria from rising in his voice...or anywhere else, for that matter. "Emily? What is this?"

The shower stopped with a metallic clank, and a slender arm reached out to yank a towel from the shelf. A moment later, Emily stepped out, all damp and steamy and alluring beneath the short wrap of terry cloth. "What?" She tucked the end of the towel into a makeshift knot above her left breast, then flipped her hair over her head and bound it into a turban with a second towel.

"This..." He stuttered and stopped, hoping his sudden speech paralysis had something to do with outrage instead of relating entirely to the fact that Emily Dawson had great legs. Really great legs. In fact, he'd had no idea how good she looked all over. Of course, he'd had no reason to even think about her body before, but he suddenly realized it was going to be quite a while before he could stop thinking about it now. In renewed self-defense, he waved the photo at her. "What in the hell is *this?*"

She stopped rubbing her hair, stopped flexing the petal-pink underside of her arms, stopped...and looked at the picture. A small frown tucked in at the corners of her lips. "Mm," she said. "Not your most attractive side, I admit, but it's a pretty good shot of me, don't you think?"

He lifted it as if he meant to examine her likeness, then stopped. "This is a damned wedding photograph."

"We can always have another one made if you're that unhappy with it."

"This is not my idea of a joke." Frowning, he tapped the picture. "People shouldn't make jokes about...well, about weddings."

She blinked, looked down, rubbed droplets of water from her ankle...a trim, nicely turned ankle at the end of a long, shapely stretch of leg. Kurt barely raised his gaze before she met his eyes. "You don't know how happy I am to hear that, Kurt. Last night...well, everything happened so fast, and I was afraid...." A breathy half-laugh escaped her. "I know it's silly, but I thought you might feel badly about not being able to...well, you know."

A wave of relief hit him. He hadn't had sex with her. He hadn't been able to— The relief vanished, replaced by a rising ego, and even though he knew things like that happened to men all the time, they had never happened to *him*. Well, okay, that once, but he'd been drunk. As drunk as last night. But that time the woman had been—hell, he couldn't even remember her name. This was *Emily*. Marshaling all the reasons he needed to be happy at having been a nonperformer, he gave her his best can't-win-'em-all grin. "Guess I'd had a few too many beers to be, uh, romantic, huh?"

He could have sworn she blushed, although her skin was still rosy from the shower. "You thought—Oh, no, Kurt, I was referring to the *wedding,* not afterward." She pressed her lips together, then smiled. "I have to tell you that that part, the *afterward,* was…" Her hands splayed as if helping her gather the words. "Well, nothing like *that* has ever happened to me before."

His ego felt better for a second…right up until one word rang a death knell inside his head. "W-wedding?" He tested the word, licked his suddenly dry lips, then tried it again. "What wedding?"

Her gaze ducked shyly away from his. "Ours, silly."

"Ours?" he repeated. "We really got…*married?*"

"Last night," she said, nodding, her lashes sweeping down, her chin slowly dipping against her chest, the very picture of a blushing bride. "It was very romantic. Don't you remember…*darlin'?*"

It was her soft repetition of his earlier endearment that knocked the stuffing out of his knees, the coy way her lashes veiled the earthy fire in her eyes that leveled his certainty that this was all some big prank. "We got—" He gulped. "—married?"

Her lips tightened, then quivered. "You don't remember?" She looked like she might burst into tears at any second. "You don't remember the most—"

her chin began to quiver "—the most *romantic* night of my entire life?"

Kurt didn't know if it was the quivering chin or the subtle mockery in the words that tipped him off. But in that instant, the game was up, and he remembered a lot of things. Mainly, how irritating Emily Dawson could be. "I may be a little thick this morning, but I know good and well that whatever we might have done last night didn't have anything to do with *romance.*"

Her chin came up faster than a calf after a branding. "We got married," she stated unequivocally. "Deal with it."

He imitated a buzzing sound. "Wrong answer, try again."

Her frown might have wowed him if he'd been able to focus on anything besides the knot of the towel…which seemed in imminent danger of coming apart. He was just imagining what he might do if it slipped when she cleared her throat. He noticed she'd dropped the blushing-bride demeanor. "You are such a cretin," she said, and came purposefully toward him.

"Just a realist." Which was the main reason he backed out of the doorway and out of her way.

"Well, Mr. Realist, as they say, a picture is worth a thousand words." She brushed past him in a snit, trailing wet footprints and the steamy scent of hotel-room shampoo.

He glanced again at the photo and followed her. "In this case, I'll take the words...all thousand of them."

"It'll just take three. We—got—married."

"No." He denied it. "No, this has to be somebody's idea of a joke because..."

"Because?"

"Because there's no way you and I would have..." Her eyebrows arched a question, and Kurt decided there was no need to be tactless. "Well, we just wouldn't have."

She sat on the edge of the mattress. The towel bunched, and Kurt wondered how he could have failed to notice those legs before now. Not that he'd seen her much in the last few years, but still... When she cleared her throat for the second time, he flinched and jerked his gaze to her face. "As hard as this may be to believe," she said, "we would and we did. It's no joke."

"But it has to be. Nellis or Sam or...or somebody put something in my drink and doctored up this photo, because there is no way in hell that I'd—"

"Careful, Kurtis, you're about to hurt my feelings."

For a moment, she had him again, and he very nearly apologized, but—*married?* To Emily? What the *hell* had they put in his drink? "Look, Emily, you've never pretended to have anything except the utmost distaste for me, so isn't it time you just came clean?''

She eyed him, then tugged off the turban and began to towel her wet hair, which in his current state of hangover distress was one of the most sensually soothing acts he'd ever watched. It struck him as oddly humorous that he'd said come clean when she so obviously was. Clean, that is. Squeaky clean from her shower. The glow still showed in the glistening ivory of her shoulders, covered in long, straight strands of very dark, very wet hair. He was an idiot not to have noticed sooner that Emily had grown up rather nicely. But then, it was beginning to look like he was an idiot all the way around.

''Okay, Kurt,'' she said in a voice at once hesitant and considering. ''I suppose since you are my husband—'' she paused to let the word give him a heart attack, then continued ''—you deserve to know the truth. Last night when you proposed, frankly, I was caught by surprise. Completely taken aback by your sudden declaration that it was me you'd really loved all those years. Not Carolina. And, well, I know I should have insisted we wait, but when you told me you'd kept silent all those years because you thought you were far too old to interest someone as young and energetic as me, well...at first I didn't believe you, but then you kept insisting, kept saying how much you cared, how much you'd *always* cared about me, how you had to act like such a consummate jerk to keep from sweeping me into your arms and carrying me into the sunset..."

Self-defense seemed called for suddenly. "I was drunk!"

Her expression informed him that was not pertinent, and her voice kept on cataloguing his purported sins. "*After* all your protestations of sincerity, *after* you convinced me that the *only* way you could ever have had the courage to tell me all this was when you'd had too much to drink, well, I was just swept off my feet and into the most incredible..." Her smile softened, turned innocent and beguiling. False, perhaps, but very beguiling. "Incredible and, yes, *romantic* night of my entire life." Her smile returned with knee-buckling shyness and, even knowing she had to be lying through her teeth, Kurt had to catch his breath. "You were simply... wonderful beyond my dreams." Her palm caressed the wrinkled sheets. "I never thought the...first time...could be so...satisfying." Here she ducked her head, and his headache became a low roar inside his head.

"Give it up, Emily. We didn't have sex and we didn't get married."

She stood up. "Yes we did. Obviously, you want to pretend you can't remember anything about it. Obviously you regret it. Well, fine! I don't want to be married to a man who is so...so shallow he'd marry me just to have his way with me." Her eyes shimmered with sudden tears that he knew in his gut were fake...but pinched his heart just the same. "I want an annulment, Kurt. Do you hear me? I want an immediate annulment so I can forget I ever, for a second, thought you weren't a total sleazeball!"

With that, she stalked into the bathroom and slammed the door, the noise reverberating in his head like a thousand clamoring words.

## Chapter Four

Emily cleared the mirror with a towel and stared wide-eyed at the woman who stared wide-eyed back at her. Then she smiled. "Emily," she said to her reflection. "When you are good, you are very, *very* good." Not that she thought he'd actually believed a word of it. He wasn't *that* big an idiot. But let him wonder. Let him worry. Let him find out for himself that their marriage was not only real, but legal. Let him think he'd taken advantage of her in his drunken state. Let him wonder if she could possibly have been a virgin. A giggle escaped her, and she muffled it into a strangled sob in case he was listening on the other side of the door. Let him think she was crying, disillusioned, the romance killed in her soul. It would do him good to hold himself accountable for last night, even if it hadn't happened the way she'd said. He deserved to wonder, and she deserved to enjoy whatever doubt she could inflict.

He knocked. "Emily?"

"Go away." She added a sniff for extra credibility. "I never want to see you again."

He repeated the knock. "Open the door, Emily. I know what this is about now, and it's not going to work."

She frowned at herself in the mirror. "What what's about?"

"This whole pretense about getting married."

"I'm not pretending."

"Oh, yes, you are, and I just figured out why."

"You wouldn't have a clue if you won it on *Wheel of Fortune.*"

"Really. Well, let me buy you a couple of vowels and put them into the two words I have for you. McCauley Khakis."

She had the door open so fast she practically set the hinges on fire. *"This,"* she said strongly, "has nothing to do with that."

His smile relaxed, signaling that he had found an angle and was going to run with it. "Yes, it does. You're trying to con me into endorsing that clothing line you want to market in your Western wear store. You set me up last night, Emily, and now you're trying to blackmail me into doing what I refused to do six months ago."

Emily was furious. Not so much because of his accusation, but because she hadn't even thought about the marriage from a commercial angle. And she called herself a businesswoman. "I would never stoop to blackmail," she said.

"You would," he replied, crossing his arms across his ridiculously broad chest. "And you did."

"Did not."

"Did, too."

"I did not."

"You did, too. Come on, Emily. Be a big girl. Confess you invented this whole wedding-night scenario to get the endorsement rights to my name."

"The name of a washed-up, has-been nobody of a rodeo bum? Ha! I wouldn't waste my breath, much less my virginity."

He leaned against the door frame, smiling still, and Emily began to understand how a woman might—under certain circumstances—fall victim to those eyes. "Well, now," he drawled. "If I'd known *that* was what you were offering, I might have given you permission to stitch my name on the hip pocket of those jeans months ago."

"They're slacks. Nice slacks, and I offered *you* a percentage of profits," she snapped. "But you didn't even have the common decency to pick up the phone and turn me down personally."

"You're the one who sent that weasely cousin of yours with the proposition."

"Carolina told me you never considered endorsements unless they were presented through a professional."

"Here's a news flash for you, Emily. Milton Meeks may be an attorney, but he is no professional, and for future reference, I don't do endorsements, no matter who presents them."

"Carolina said you would."

"Well, Carolina didn't ask me, did she?"

Emily was sorry she'd mentioned her sister's name. "Oh, so you'd do it for her, but not for me…your wife?"

His smug expression altered with frustration. "For the last time, Emily, give it up. You are not my wife. I may have had too much to drink last night and I may not be able to remember much at the moment, but this hangover will go away, I will remember what happened, and you're going to feel like an idiot for lying."

"I already feel like an idiot," she said. "For thinking I was doing you a favor."

"A favor? You think marrying me was a *favor?*"

"I don't care if you believe me or not." She sniffed, just so he'd remember that she was the injured party. "I saved your sorry butt last night, and you owe me, McCauley. You owe me, big-time."

"I see," he said with a nod. "So, how many times do I have to have sex with you to pay this debt?"

Oh, he was cocky, but she would wipe that obnoxious expression off his face one way or another.

"Last night should never have happened…and for the record, I didn't enjoy it."

He regarded her with a sad little frown. "You know, I always did kind of admire your stubborn streak, Emily, but you can't go around claiming to be married when you're not…or to have had sex with a fella when you didn't."

"And why is it so impossible for you to believe I could be telling the truth?"

"Because I couldn't get drunk enough to do something that stupid."

She stiffened. "And the something that stupid would be what? Marrying me or sleeping with me?"

He hesitated, but not long. "Getting married…but I'm also smart enough not to have unprotected sex."

"We were in heat," she told him, stung by his holier-than-thou tone. "You never even *thought* about protection."

"And you expect me to believe it never occurred to you, the *virgin,* either?"

She sniffed. "I'm on the pill…for personal reasons. So long as you don't have some nasty little germs, I'm safe."

"You wouldn't take that chance, Emily. Not with me. We didn't have sex, we didn't get married, and there's nothing you can say that will convince me we did."

She regarded him with an acute mixture of disappointment and disgust. Why she was disgusted was an easy call. Why she was disappointed wasn't. It had to be, she decided, his continued and arrogant belief that he would never, under any circumstances, consider her as a sexual partner. Not that he was on her short list, either, but he didn't have to act as if the whole idea was completely repugnant.

She snagged the wedding picture from his hand and pointed to the printed label on the back. "Here's the name of the wedding chapel," she said. "Why don't you give them a call? Then try the courthouse. I'm sure it's listed in the phone book. If you need further confirmation, call a few of your drinking buddies...Nellis or Kipp. No, forget them, they probably don't remember much more than you do. Call Genna or Jeannie...or better yet, call Farrah Phillips and ask her how *she's* feeling this morning. Then, when it finally gets through your wooden skull that I'm *not* lying, you can contact my weasely cousin, Milton, because from this moment on, you'll have to get a professional to present any propositions you may have for me!"

He caught the door before she could swing it shut in his obnoxious face, dwarfing her with his superior height and aggravation. He grabbed her hand and pulled her through the doorway and toward the bed. "Humor me," he said. "Let's make these phone calls together, *wife*."

"McCAULEY, YES. And Dawson. Emily Dawson." Kurt smiled at Emily, clearly in the grip of self-righteous vindication. "Yes, I'll wait." He covered the mouthpiece with his palm. "She's going to check the license applications."

Emily nodded from her perch on the edge of the bed, where she was digging her toes into the carpet and wishing she'd gotten dressed before getting into this double-dog-dare showdown. Of course, it was a tad late to feel embarrassed about sitting around in a towel while her soon-to-be-annulled husband paced back and forth in his pin-striped boxers. It was also, she supposed, a little late for the unvarnished truth. At this point, she didn't think he'd believe her no matter what she said. Then again, it was his own fault if he couldn't remember what had or hadn't happened.

"There is?" Kurt's heretofore complacent tone snapped to smart attention. "Would you mind checking it again?" A weighty pause. "You don't have to *read* it to me…okay…you're absolutely positive it's spelled the same?" Another pause, this time with his back turned. "Well, of course, I remember," he said into the receiver. "I'm just checking to make sure it's all legal." His grip on the phone was white-knuckled. "No, she didn't *lie* about her age! Look, thanks for looking it up…yes, thank you…we'll look forward to receiving the marriage license in the mail." He dropped the phone onto the base with a clatter and dropped onto the bed next to Emily. "We're married," he said flatly.

"I knew that," she answered.

"It's legal, too."

"I was pretty sure it was." She paused. "You paid them cash."

He leaned back, putting his hands behind his head, staring at the ceiling, his muscular bare legs sprawled next to hers, also bare. His chest was bare, too. Bronzed, broad and bare. It occurred to her that today was the first time in a long time she'd been this close to a naked—or nearly naked—man, the first time in recent memory that she'd been this close to being naked *with* a nearly naked man. Not that this morning counted. Not even close. Still, she wished she'd had a razor so she could have shaved her legs. Nonchalantly, she cupped her hands over the unsightly stubble on her knees before she glanced at him. "Cheer up, McCauley," she said. "It could be worse."

He rolled his head, swinging his gaze to her. "I don't rightly see how."

Feeling a little sorry for him, she leaned over to tap him on the chin. "You could be in Nova Scotia by now."

He captured her hand, flipped her onto her back faster than she could utter a surprised oof, and pinned her beneath him. "I don't know how you did this, Emily, but you are gonna tell me everything that happened last night before I let you up from here.''

He was heavy. Warm. Male. Oh, yeah, very male. She wrangled a bit of resentment at his high-handedness, a touch of outrage for his rough handling, a hint of scorn for his anger…but it was a struggle to corral a rather lovely thrill at being so close to so much testosterone. "And if I refuse?" she asked, unarmed and unafraid.

"We're gonna be in this hotel a real long time," he said smoothly.

"Are you threatening me?"

"Nope. Just telling you how it's gonna be."

"I'm not scared of you," she said, even as she realized what she *was* scared of—the loosening knot on her towel wrap. Going absolutely still, she avoided an immediate disrobement and decided the sooner she told the truth, the sooner she could snatch her dignity from the jaws of disaster. "Okay," she said in a rush. "Here's what happened. You got drunk. You became first prize in a marriage raffle. You were won by three-times-at-bat Farrah Phillips. You were hot to marry her. I drove. We stopped at the courthouse for the license. You were suddenly hot to marry me. Farrah loves community property laws. Voilà! A last-minute bride swap. Wedding chapel. Brief ceremony. Boom. Here we are. Any questions?"

His frown was less intimidating up close. "That's it?"

"In a nutshell. Don't you remember *anything?*"

"I remember why I stopped hanging out with that bunch of knuckleheads."

"Except for last night."

He winced. "Yeah, except for then. Are you sure no one put anything in my drink?"

"Limes, but I'm pretty sure they weren't toxic. I mean, lots of people had limes, and nobody else got married."

He winced.

"I let them raffle me off like some prize turkey?"

"Just like a turkey," she said, loving the sound of that. "You seemed to think it was a gesture of defiance toward all women."

His sigh was deep and heartfelt. "I don't think I've ever been *that* drunk before."

She started to shrug, but stopped as she felt the towel slip again. "Well, you did have a broken heart."

"I did?"

"I *know* you remember that part."

"In the overall ache this morning, I haven't given my heart much attention."

"What do you know? The remedy worked."

He groaned and fell back, releasing her and her dignity.

Her hands flew to secure the towel around her.

"If it makes you feel any better, a lot of women bought raffle tickets."

"How many did you spring for?"

"Zero. Zilch. Nada." She stood up, looked at him lying there in his wrinkled boxers, looking miserable and sort of lost and—darn it, more than a little attractive—and she felt an unexpected twinge of sympathy for his troubles. "Are you kidding? I was afraid if I bought even one, I'd win. And then what would I do with you?"

"Marry me and blackmail me into an endorsement with the divorce settlement."

Sympathy vanished in the realization that she was *married* to this lecherous bag of aches and pains and that this was not the way to get *unmarried*. "I don't want a divorce, Kurt. I want an annulment. I want this horrendous lapse in judgment to skulk off into the annals of the Knucklehead Gang. I want it erased, wiped out, expunged and expurgated from the record books and my memory."

"You don't want an annulment half as badly as I do."

"You're right. I want it twice as much as you do. A trillion times more."

He pushed upright, hands braced on the edge of the mattress. "Then what are we doing here?" he said. "Let's get the ball and chain rolling toward the locksmith."

"Fine." She headed for the bathroom and her clothes. "I'll be ready in ten minutes."

"I'll be ready in five."

She stopped at the bathroom door, furious beyond reason, frustrated past the point of caring why. "You are such a knot head, McCauley. It isn't as if you can get the annulment without me, you know."

"I wouldn't dream of it. You got me into this, Emily, and you're the one who's going to get me out of it."

"I should have let Farrah have you. Then you wouldn't be such a loudmouth this morning."

"I know how to handle women like Farrah." He arched his brows in that lecherous way of his, his mouth all but disappearing into that dreadful mustache. "It's *virgins* that give me trouble."

"As your most recent *conversion*, I can vouch for that!"

"Oh, come on, Emily, if I was so drunk I *married* you, I was way too drunk to have sex, much less with someone as inexperienced as you!"

"Who said I was inexperienced?"

"You're saying you're an *experienced* virgin?"

She obviously was getting too caught up in this argument. "For your information, I do a lot of reading. And it's just like a man to change the subject. Don't keep trying to distract me, Kurt. It only makes you look like an insensitive jerk."

It was his turn to blink. "I'm an insensitive jerk?

You trick me into marriage for your own very commercial purposes, have sex with me while I'm unconscious, and *I'm* an insensitive jerk?''

"No, Kurtis. You're an insensitive jerk because you have turned something that could have been beautiful and romantic into some—some sordid blackmail scheme.'' She stepped into the bathroom, once again in the driver's seat. "And it would serve you right if I took advantage of this awful situation and used your hateful name in an endorsement.''

"Oh, sure. Right.'' He followed her to the doorway, frustration in every nuance of movement and voice. "I am on to you, Emily Dawson. I don't know how you got the license, I don't know how you got me to go through a ceremony and I sure as hell don't know how you were able to seduce me into having sex with you—if, in fact, you did—but I do know why. So don't try to con me into thinking this was somehow my fault.''

Emily hadn't known he could be so stubborn. To think she'd always believed that it would take less than five minutes and even less energy to verbally knock him into Kingdom Come. "I was wrong, Kurt,'' she said in a quite reasonable tone. "You're not an insensitive jerk. You're an insensitive idiot.'' She started to close the door, then paused. "And only my friends call me Emily. In future, if you must talk to me, I'd appreciate it if you'd call me by my legal name. That would be *Mrs.* Kurtis McCauley, to you.''

Then she slammed the door.

KURT GOT DRESSED under a thundercloud. The words he wanted to say streaked across his brain like lightning bolts, the headache he wished would go away pounded like a torrential rain, an overall irritation stung him like hail. How could sweet, affable, delightful Carolina be blood related to that...that woman? How could that cute, gawky kid he remembered as Carolina's pesky little sister have grown up to be so conniving and lying-through-her-teeth cunning? He shoved his shirttail into his jeans and dropped to all fours to look under the bed for his missing sock.

Now, what in hell had she done with it? Flattening out, he stuck his arm almost up to the shoulder into the narrow space between the bed frame and the floor and felt around for the missing sock. Nothing, damn it. He'd have to wear one boot without a sock, which would rub at least one blister, probably several, one of which would undoubtedly get infected, meaning he could lose an entire foot, thanks to Emily Dawson and her conniving. Getting angrier by the minute, he jerked his arm from under the bed, twisting it into the bargain. ''Ow!'' he said as he sat up—and banged his head on the bedside table. ''Ow! Damn it!''

Emily stepped out of the bathroom, still wearing that skimpy towel, and looked at him from the other side of the bed. "Are you okay?"

"What do you care?" He rubbed both shoulder and head, feeling sorrier for himself by the second. "And what did you do with my sock?"

Her eyebrows lifted, and damn it, if that didn't make her long legs look even longer. "Well, for one thing, I don't want you to die before I can get this stupid marriage annulled. And for another, I would never touch your socks."

"Well, I can't find it."

"Did you look in the sheets?"

"No, I didn't look in the sheets," he said with attitude. "I wouldn't get into bed with one sock on."

She sniffed. "As I said, you were in a hurry."

"Hmph," he said, as it was the only response that came to mind. "A likely story."

She—and her long legs—came around the bed, stopped with the curves of her knees tantalizingly close to his face—close enough that he could smell the floral scent of the lotion she'd probably only moments ago rubbed on her skin. Her arm snaked under the rumpled sheets and came out with a sock, which she dangled in front of him before dropping it like a stinky worm. "You owe me double for this, Kurt."

"Forget it. I think I'm entitled to a few little perks out of this marriage."

"On second thought, maybe I would rather be a widow."

A knock saved him from something—he wasn't sure what—and as Emily turned to look at the door, Kurt managed to get to his feet without incurring further injury. He zipped his jeans as he moved past her, reluctantly acknowledging again that faint, soft scent of lotion that seemed to cling to her skin. "I'll get it," he said. "Seeing as how you aren't dressed for company."

"Maybe I can't find my underwear," she snapped.

"Well, it's not under the bed," he snapped in turn as he slid back the safety chain and the dead bolt. Obviously, he hadn't been so drunk last night—or in such a hurry—that he'd forgotten to secure the door. Surely that was one point for the insensitive jerk's theory that nothing had happened. Well, except for the marriage license. And it was possible that she'd bribed a few public officials along the way, he thought as he opened the door.

"Kurtis McCauley? Are you Kurt McCauley?" A pretty young woman in a newscaster's blue suit smiled at him. Beside her a pretty young man in short sleeves and slacks sported an equally delighted grin.

"Did you marry Emily Dawson last night?" His

eager words practically trampled the woman's. "At the Lovebird Lane Wedding Chapel?"

"Well, that's her story," he answered.

The spiffy-looking couple laughed. Kurt offered them his best and fiercest frown, but the pair's enthusiasm was undaunted. "Mr. McCauley," the young man began but—just like a female—Ms. Blue Suit finished his sentence for him.

"This is your lucky day!"

Her voice, pitched high with excitement, caused yet more brain cells to bounce to their deaths in the hangover that still had command of Kurt's head.

"You, sir," the young man informed him proudly, "are a winner!"

Kurt decided he'd had more than enough excitement for one morning and started to shut the door in their smiling faces. Emily, however, ducked under his arm and came up in its circle. "What did we win?" she asked and Kurt really wanted to point out that no one had said anything about *we*. Of course, as the *husband*, he didn't get a chance.

"Mrs. McCauley? Are you Mrs. Kurtis McCauley?" The litany of name-calling started again.

"Yes," Emily agreed eagerly, then repeated, "what did we win?"

The woman's smile remained steady, but the young man's grew by leaps and bounds when his gaze dropped to the skimpy little towel that barely covered Emily. Kurt dropped his arm protectively around her bare shoulders and attempted to draw her inside. "If you don't mind," he said politely to Tweedledee and Dum. "We're sort of, uh, occupied, right now."

"No, we're not." Emily held her ground but didn't shrug off his arm. "We were just having a fight."

The smiles dimmed. Well, the woman's did. The man was still appraising Emily appreciatively. "Uh-oh," the woman said. "Fighting the day after your wedding?" She shook her head, then glanced at the man. "Make a note of that, Rodney."

"Righto, Ange." Rodney made an apparent note of Emily's measurements, instead.

Kurt thought the guy had shifty eyes, too. "Make a note of what?" Kurt tightened his grip on Emily, giving Rodney as many hands-off warnings as he could without punching the guy in midleer.

"Marital discord," Rodney said, as if that explained everything, including his inability to stop ogling Kurt's wife.

"Oh, it wasn't a real fight," Emily said, patting Kurt's stomach a little harder than was necessary. "He was just looking for his underwear."

"Sock," Kurt corrected, covering her patting hand with his and giving it a testy squeeze. "I lost a sock."

"Oh, a *sock*." Ange's smile beamed as brightly as a fresh idea. "Well, in that case, I suppose I can tell you that I'm Angela Abbott and this is Rodney Ricker and we work for radio station KLAS here in Las Vegas, and Mr. and Mrs. McCauley, today is your lucky day! You're the winning newlyweds in KLAS's Ring in the Weddings and Win a Classic contest! You've just won a classic, mint-condition 1965 Mustang convertible!''

Eyes shining, Emily looked at Kurt. He looked at her—and decided he would let her have the endorsement if she would let him keep the car.

## Chapter Five

"Every other weekend and alternate holidays," Emily said. "And that's my final offer."

Elbow on the window rest, headache in hand, Kurt regarded her from the passenger seat of the classic convertible that was now, dubiously, *theirs.* "We are not sharing custody of this car, no matter how many offers you make."

"I don't see why not. It's the civilized way to handle the situation." The wind coming across the windshield whipped her hair about her face as she smiled at him. "We didn't have any problem deciding who would drive home."

"Only because you won the coin toss and there were photographers everywhere taking our picture," he said shortly. "The *civilized* way to handle that situation would have been for you to drive your van and for me to drive this car."

"I can go back for the van anytime. Possession is nine-tenths of the law, and you're crazy if you think I was going to let you snatch this wonderful car out from under me.''

"I've already offered to buy your half. Fair market value.''

"Fair market, my foot. There isn't another car like this one in the world. It's mint. It only has twelve thousand original miles on it, for Pete's sake. I'm not selling my half, and I don't have the cash to buy yours, so we're just going to have to negotiate custody.''

"We're just going to have to sell the car and split the money.''

"We can't do that, either. We signed that affidavit for the radio station agreeing we wouldn't sell the car for six months so they get their money's worth out of running those we-were-winners-on-Classic-KLAS radio ads.''

"We didn't sign anything that said we can't give it back.''

"Are you kidding? We are not giving it back. The radio station doesn't want it. They'd have to do another whole contest, take all those silly pictures again with some other couple, change their ad campaign. Wouldn't be cost-efficient.'' She turned her head toward him, her hair blowing across her shoulder in a long, enthusiastic wave. "Do you think they'll mention the store when they make the announcement that we won? That could be good.''

Kurt, frankly, didn't see much good in any of the

events that had occupied the past twenty-four hours. "If they don't mention Dawson's Duds, it won't be because you failed to let them know about it," he said, testy with hangover. "You were a walking, talking commercial."

"If you hadn't been so stuck-up six months ago, you could have been *wearing* an advertisement and sharing the profits."

He thought she grossly overcalculated the popularity of his name stitched on the seat of a pair of pants, but hell if he was going to say so. "You married me, Emily. That entitles me to a share of the profits, anyway."

"Ha! Don't even consider stepping foot inside my store unless you're going to buy something."

"No problem...as long as you stay out of my car."

"*Your* car? Ha, again! If it wasn't for me, we wouldn't even be having this conversation."

"True, I'd be having it with Farrah. And she'd let me have the car."

"Dream on. She'd take the car and every other possession you own. Face it, McCauley, you're lucky I was willing to save your bacon last night. The least you can do is let me keep the car."

"I thought you wanted the endorsement."

She turned her head toward him, her lips curving with a calculating sunniness. "Okay, if you insist,

I'll take that, too. But that's all. I won't accept another blessed thing from you.''

He shook his head, amused despite his better judgment. ''I can't believe Carolina never warned me about what a little opportunist you are.''

''Like Carolina would have noticed…even if I was, which I'm not.'' She gathered a handful of hair and tucked it behind her ear, where it promptly escaped to blow about her face again. ''I'm always going to drive with the top down.''

''Convertibles are a pain when it rains.''

''The air-conditioning is going in the van.''

''Classic cars have to be washed and waxed every other day. Sometimes more often.''

''The van is really on its last leg, and I can't afford to keep pouring money into fixing it.''

''Classic cars require constant maintenance.''

''I have to have something else to drive.''

Kurt stopped watching the float of hair about her shoulders, shifted his attention to the determined set of her chin, decided to nip her fantasy in the bud. ''I'm not giving up my interest in this car,'' he said. ''And I'm not sharing it with you, either. No matter how bad a shape your van is in.''

Her lips tightened. ''You don't have a very positive attitude, Kurtis, and that could interfere with the process of obtaining a speedy annulment. I'll have to ask Cousin Milton.''

''You do that,'' he said, and then because he felt

out of sorts and knew it would rile her, he added, "darlin'."

Like a magnetic force, the one word brought her gaze to his in a simmer. "Don't call me that," she said tightly. "It's annoying, patronizing and offensive."

He rubbed the flat of his thumb along his temple, pleased to have aggravated her so easily. "It's just a word."

"It's an endearment, and as I don't find you endearing, it'd be best if you kept words like that for your little rodeo groupies."

He very nearly grinned. "That almost sounds like a threat, Emily. What are you going to do if I keep calling you darlin'? Sic your boyfriend on me?"

She eyed him coolly. "I wouldn't do that, Kurtis. He's so much younger than you, it wouldn't be a fair fight."

"Younger, huh?" Kurt drawled. "Does he have his driver's license yet? Because I don't want you letting some lead-footed kid behind the wheel of my Mustang."

She tossed him a dazzling smile…and his elbow slid off the window rest. "Another reason I should have the car," she said easily. "I'm obviously the more responsible driver. I would never let anyone else drive our prize convertible. You'll be letting Nellis and Kipp and the rest of those idiots in the driver's seat."

"Nope. Just me. One set of keys, and they stay in my pocket."

"Sorry. I'll be keeping them in my purse."

He looked at the saucy set of her lips and wondered why he'd never realized how pretty she was. Not as beautiful as Carolina, certainly, but still a very attractive young woman. And she did have legs worth writing home about. "We're getting an annulment, Emily, which means one of us has to give up the car—gracefully."

"That would be the gentlemanly thing to do."

"True, but then women are more mature than men."

She sighed, frowned, flipped the sun visor up, then down again. "I guess we'll just give the car back, then."

"Yep. Guess we will."

"Shame. Especially considering that the radio station spent a lot of money on those pictures today. Rodney said he'd send copies to me."

Kurt tried to look impressed. "An accommodating guy, that Rodney."

"Yes, he is." She kept her eyes on the road. "A real gentleman. He'd let me have the car."

"Only because he saw you in terry cloth."

"I beg your pardon?"

"The man saw you wearing a towelette. He wants to impress you."

"*You* saw me in a towel," she pointed out, "and it certainly hasn't made a gentleman out of you."

"That's different. We're married."

The earthy fire returned to her eyes. "I'm starting to think I want the car, the endorsement *and* alimony."

"I'm starting to think McCauley's Duds has a nice ring to it."

Her sigh echoed frustration. "You might at least entertain the notion of sharing the car with me. I know we could work out a suitable arrangement."

"We have trouble sharing the same sky, Emily. What makes you think we wouldn't murder each other over this damn car?"

Her pause was just long enough to acknowledge the truth of that before her words denied it. "I can get along with you if I want to. You're the one with the bad attitude."

Kurt saw an opening and took it. "How much are you willing to bet?"

She arched an eyebrow. "That you have a bad attitude? Anything you want to wager. That's a sure bet if I ever heard one."

"Forget my attitude," he said. "How much are you willing to bet you can get along with me?"

"For the rest of my life? Nothing. For a couple of weeks?" She snapped her fingers. "I can do that in my sleep."

Probably the only way she could, he thought. This

would be like taking candy from a baby. "So? What are you willing to bet?"

"Your half of the car?" she suggested.

"Against your half of the car?"

She hesitated, maybe sensing a trap, but then took the bait. "Sure. We'll share the car for two weeks, and at the end of the second week you'll sign over your half of the car, and it'll belong to me."

"Providing you don't lose your temper during the two weeks." He knew she'd never last a day, much less fourteen of them. "But this has to be a real contest. We spend the next two weeks together. Morning, noon, night. Winner take all."

"Wait just a minute, cowboy. Morning, noon and…" she began, then stopped. "Winner take all as in the car *and* the endorsement?"

"Yep."

"What do you want out of this deal?"

"The car and free duds from your store for as long as I want."

"I won't lose, Kurt."

"I think you will, Emily."

Her lips curved smugly. "I suppose even insensitive jerks are entitled to their opinion. But, no matter what happens, we still get the annulment."

"Goes without saying," he said. "So is it a bet?"

She drove for a minute without saying anything, then, "We spend the next two weeks together, and whoever cries uncle first loses. What if it's a toss-up?"

Like that was going to happen. She'd be throwing up her hands within twenty-four hours. "Then we'll share custody of the car, but no endorsement and no free clothes."

She pursed her lips, deliberating. "So you'd move in with me for the two weeks?"

"You'll move in with me."

"Oh, no. I don't think so. It was your idea. You come to my house."

"I come with an entourage of animals. You don't. Makes more sense to stay at the ranch."

Argument was on the tip of her tongue. He knew it was, but she caught the objections, considered the prize and nodded. "Okay, Kurtis, you've got yourself a bet."

He hated it when she called him that, but saying so would only insure she kept it up. With a smile, he extended his hand. "It's a bet," he said, and waited until she accepted the handshake before he added in his best and most endearing drawl, "darlin'."

TWO WEEKS. Emily pulled half a dozen outfits from her closet and wondered what she'd been thinking when she agreed to such a ridiculous proposal. She wanted to keep the car, sure, and she wanted that endorsement, but she should never have let Kurt lure her into making a bet about it. Even if she knew she'd win. Even if there wasn't a doubt in her mind that she could survive being in the same house with him. Even if the grand prize was more than worth the inconvenience of staying at his ranch.

She zipped the clothes into a hanging bag and went into the bathroom to gather her toiletries. No doubt about it. Something in the air at the Silver Dollar Cowboy Saloon must have entered her brain last night and gobbled up her common sense. In barely twenty-four hours, she'd stepped up to the altar with, shared a hotel room with, won a contest with and made an insane bet with Kurt McCauley, the only man she knew who could raise her blood pressure five points just by having a mustache that needed trimming. And now she was packing to spend two whole weeks with him! Crazy, crazy, crazy. Just the thought of it had her adrenaline pumping like a maniacal bodybuilder.

Dumping her makeup into a travel bag, she wondered if he'd have such essentials as shampoo and toothpaste, then automatically reached for her own, not eager to share one thing more than was absolutely necessary. She certainly hoped his run-down ranch house had more than one bathroom. That could be a deal breaker right there, she thought as she grabbed a can of Lysol and tucked it between the shampoo bottle and the tube of bath gel. If Kurt thought for a minute that she was going to clean up after him, he was in for a rude awakening.

The crash of breaking glass set her teeth on edge, and she marched toward the kitchen, certain he'd broken something priceless and irreplaceable and probably on purpose. Just to get her all riled up before the bet even got started. But when she saw him standing in the midst of her scattered collection of silverware, holding a cabinet drawer in his hand and looking attractively embarrassed, her irritation faded. "I was going to make coffee," he said. "But the drawer stuck, and when I pulled on it..." He looked at the forks, spoons and knives on the floor.

"It does that all the time." She opened the cabinet door above the stove where she kept the coffee makings. "I've been meaning to call someone out to fix it."

"Got a candle?"

"Why? Are you going to black out?"

"No, I'm going to fix your drawer." As he bent and began scooping silverware off the floor, he tossed a persuasive smile at her. "And all I'll charge for my skill and ingenuity is a cup of coffee."

"Deal," she said, and smiled back. "Providing I can find a candle."

She found one, then made coffee while he rubbed the candle along the glide strips and within a few minutes had the drawer sliding with ease. "There." He gave it another test pull, then straightened and solemnly handed her the candle. "Save this. It may be the only thing standing between you and disaster."

"Oh, no," she assured him. "I've got plenty of duct tape. And if that won't do it, I've got the miracle fix—hair spray."

He grimaced. "Do me a favor and don't fix anything at my house."

She smiled and thrust an empty coffee cup into his hand. "Fine. At your house, you fix the coffee."

"Hope you like it thick, black and strong, because that's the way I make it."

It was her turn to grimace. "In that case, a little hair spray couldn't hurt it." She turned toward the door, feeling an odd impulse to settle in with him in the kitchen, drink coffee that was made correctly—with a good measure of water, added milk and sugar—and exchange fixes for various and sundry problems. As if she and Kurt could agree on how to fix a hangnail. She needed to gather the rest of her things and fast forward through the two weeks of their bet. No friendly chats over coffee. No pleasant comparisons of how-to techniques. No imagining this man was being nice for any reason other than that he wanted full ownership of her car. And it would be hers. She would not allow Kurt McCauley to beat her at this game.

As she started across the dining room, Emily noticed the message light on her answering machine.

Without thinking, she clicked it on and waited as the tape whirred to the beginning. "Emily!" Genna's voice was first up. "Where are you, woman? Jeannie and I have a bet on what time you got home last night. She says three a.m., but I'm hoping you got lucky, got laid and haven't made it in yet. Either way, call me the second you get this message. I'm at Jeannie's. We want details, Em, and if you slept with him, we're jealous. Happy for you, of course, but jealous as all get out."

The connection clicked off, the machine beeped and Mary Lynn's voice came on. "Emily, honey, call me. It's all over town that you and Kurt tied the knot last night. Got hitched. Did the deed. Renetta says Farrah Phillips is fit to be tied. So what happened and did you sleep with him? Inquiring minds need to know. Call me."

Another click, another beep. "Emily?" Oh, no. Mother. "I just had the strangest call from your sister. One of her friends called her—on her honeymoon, mind you—to tell her that you had married Kurt McCauley. Your dad laughed when she told him, said it was more likely you'd filled his britches with buckshot, but you know Carolina, she gets hysterical over the silliest things. I just thought you ought to know, in case she calls you. Oh, and Dad wants me to tell you to come by one night this week for supper. We love you. Bye."

That call ended, and then Carolina was up. "Emily. Are you trying to ruin my honeymoon?" A laugh. "As if Kurt would have married you just to spite me. Don't worry about it, sweetie. I'm certain it's just a vicious rumor and will die down of its own accord." Another laugh, lighter this time, more assured. "I mean, it isn't as if it could be true. Be home in ten days. Jon and I are having the most incredible time. Wish you were here." Laughter again. "Well, not really. See you soon and—trust me—you want to stay as far away from Kurt as possible. He's only toying with you, Emily, because truth be told, I know he's still in love with me and, well, you *are* my sister. I'll call you the minute we get back to the States." The machine clicked, beeped and whirred as the tape rewound.

Emily knew that Kurt had heard it all. She supposed she could have turned off the machine at any point, but if the rumors were flying, he had as much right to know what was being said as she. Besides, if she had to listen to Carolina insist that the only reason Kurt would ever pay her, Emily, any attention was to get even with Carolina for marrying someone else, then he should have to hear it, too. Especially since Emily was now, in fact, his *wife*.

"The town is going to have a field day with this," she said, not ready to face him, unwilling to see if hearing Carolina's message had broken his heart anew. Not that she minded if he suffered a little, she just didn't want to witness any genuine pain. "Especially when I move in with you."

"You want to call off the bet?"

"Are you kidding?" She spun around, wondering if he actually believed she would give up without a fight. "You are not winning that car, McCauley, and you're certainly not going to get it by default."

He straightened, his hands full of spoons. "Can't blame a guy for trying. What are you going to tell your folks?"

"That I got drunk and stupid and woke up married to you, I guess." She made a face. "Seems like as good a story as any."

"Why don't you tell them the story about how I swept you off your feet?"

"They know I wouldn't be *that* stupid."

"But you did marry me, so…" His voice came very close to turning the statement into a question, making it clear he was still fishing for exactly what had happened last night.

"So?" she repeated. "My parents will come closer to believing that I married you while inebriated than that I fell for some romantic mumbo jumbo."

"Which, in fact, you did. Didn't you?"

She lifted her shoulders in a dainty shrug. "Yeah," she said. "Go figure."

"I'm trying but not having much luck." He paused, dropped a handful of spoons into the dishwasher, then shot her an appraising look. "What are you going to tell Carolina?"

Now, there was a loaded question…and it blew a hole in Emily's spirits. After all her effort to avoid Carolina's men, here she was married to the worst of the lot *and* about to take up residence with him. "I haven't thought about it." Which was a big fat lie. "What are you going to tell her?"

"The truth…soon as I remember it."

"Well, don't exhaust yourself in the effort. Carolina will make her own truth out of this, regardless of what either one of us has to say about it."

"She always claimed you were jealous of her."

Direct hit, Emily acknowledged, although jealousy had never been her real issue with Carolina. "She likes to believe that everyone wants what she has. She especially likes to think that goes double for me. But don't kid yourself, Kurt. I did not marry you to spite my sister."

"For the record, I didn't marry you to spite her, either." His forehead creased with a frown. "But then, considering that I don't remember marrying you in the first place, what the heck do I know?" Sighing, he picked up the rest of the silverware and stashed it in the dishwasher. "We have ten days to figure out what to tell Carolina," he said. "In the meantime, whatever you decide to tell your folks, I'll back you up. I'll even go with you to tell them. But right now, I'm going to pour myself a cup of coffee...even though it looks too weak to do me any good. Want some?''

"No, thanks." His offer of support with her parents was an unlooked for courtesy, probably complete with an ulterior motive. But at the moment, she'd take what she could get. "I just have to grab a couple more things, then I'm ready to go."

"No need to pack much," he told her, his attention on filling the cup with coffee. "I'm sure you'll be home before this time tomorrow."

She gave her hair a saucy toss. "Oh, don't give up so easily, Kurt. Humility doesn't suit you."

He raised his mug to her. "Here's to humility," he said with a grin. "May the best man win."

"She fully intends to." Smiling, Emily turned to go.

"Aren't you going to call your friends? Give them the intimate details of our wedding night?"

"They're imagining better details than I could give them. And no matter what I say, no one is ever going to believe I didn't sleep with you."

"I believe you."

She wasn't going to let him off the hook that easily. "Yes, well, you're the only other person who knows what really happened. I'm telling everyone else that you were too drunk to...well, you know."

"Life would be simpler if I'd been too drunk to say I do."

"But then I wouldn't have this great new car,"

she said brightly. "Every cloud has its silver lining, you know."

"Yeah, I suppose I can be glad I didn't get drunk and wake up as mayor."

She laughed. Carolina may have broken his heart, but Emily didn't think it was going to scar. And even if she never lived down the gossip, at least she'd have the satisfaction of winning this bet. Every time Kurt saw her driving the convertible, he'd be reminded that she'd beaten him fair and square. Every time she ran into him after this, she'd taste the thrill of victory. Kurt McCauley deserved to suffer for pulling her ponytail all those years ago and for getting drunk and married last night and for a bunch of other stuff she couldn't even remember at the moment. Silly as the bet might be, Emily was going to do her best to kill him with kindness during the duration of their contest. No matter how awful his coffee tasted.

HER CHEERFUL RESOLVE lasted for all of the twenty-minute drive out to the ranch, despite Kurt's attempts to goad her into an argument over the amount of personal paraphernalia she was carting to his house. She maintained her good mood while Kurt got out of the convertible to open the gate at the main entrance to the ranch, although she did consider driving off and leaving him to walk the rest of the way. But as he'd probably consider that a failure to get along, she waited with a smile for him to get into the car before she drove up the long, dusty road to the ranch house.

In the late twilight, the house looked better than she'd expected, although to be fair, she hadn't expected much. She sat looking at it, vaguely aware of Kurt's soft whistle as he got out of the car. Suddenly there was a thunderous pounding, and Emily turned her head as an enormous black horse barreled up to her side of the convertible. He slid to a stop barely an inch from the car door and dipped his head into the space between her and the steering wheel. He made a whuffing sound, dousing her in his warm, horsey breath.

"Hank! Show some manners." Kurt's voice brought a disgusted humph from the horse, who only brought his velvety nose closer to nuzzle Emily's breast pocket. This was Kurt's horse, all right.

She reached up and gave Hank a smart little thump on the nose, causing him to back off with an offended snort. "I'm delighted to meet you, Hank," she said pleasantly. "But my pockets are by invitation only."

"I'm sorry." Kurt came around the car and looped an arm around the horse's neck. "He lives on the hope that strangers carry strawberries in their pockets." He rubbed Hank's nose affectionately. "He'll do nearly anything for a strawberry."

"Me, too," Emily said, opening the door and

slipping out of the car. "But I'm pretty particular about who snuffles my pockets."

"What can I tell you? He's shameless. And I'll warn you right now that he roams this place at will. There isn't a gate on the ranch he can't either open or figure a way around or over it. Some days I think I should have named him Houdini."

Suddenly, a small white-and-brown dog raced out of the house, barking excitedly, and flung its wiry body into Kurt's arms in a frenzy of greeting. "Hello, Melba. Did you miss me?" Kurt crooned as the dog licked his face, the air, his ear and generally covered him in welcome. When Hank nudged Kurt with his nose, vying for attention, Melba snapped at the horse before returning to the serious business of greeting her master.

Emily crossed her arms at her chest, recalling the good things she'd heard about Kurt's talent as a trainer. These two obviously worshiped him. Of course, they were dumb animals. What did they know? Still, the besotted expression on his face left no doubt of his affection for them, and Emily allowed her opinion of him to edge up a few notches. It would go even higher if he'd rub her belly like he was rubbing Melba's.

Emily lassoed that wayward line of thought and gave it a where-in-heck-did-you-come-from yank. As if her belly wasn't *so* off-limits to Kurt McCauley. Wasn't it bad enough she was going to have to spend the next fourteen nights under his roof? She did not need to start having random idiotic thoughts. Giving the car a pat, she glanced around for a garage. Hmm. "Where does the convertible sleep?" she asked.

Kurt put Melba on the ground and offered Hank an unseen treat from the palm of his hand. "Right here?" he suggested.

"I don't think so," she answered just as pleasantly. "Classic cars have to be washed and waxed every other day, I believe is what you said."

"And I stand by that remark. It's obvious in this climate you can't let the dust just sit there. Could ruin the paint."

She slammed the car door with complete composure. "You're not letting my car sit outside overnight," she told him firmly. "Either it goes in the barn or in the living room. Makes no difference to me."

His frown all but conceded the first battle of wills. "There's a garage on the other side of the house. Give me the keys, and I'll drive it around."

She thought about insisting on driving it around herself, making certain there actually was a garage back there. But she was ninety-nine percent positive that Kurt wouldn't leave the car out no matter how hard he tried to make her think otherwise. And really, there was nothing to be gained by gloating. They both knew who was ahead in this game. They both knew who was going to win. She stepped forward to give him the keys, and Melba growled low in her throat. Emily looked from terrier to owner. "Have I done something to offend your dog?"

"Melba! Heel." Kurt spoke softly but with authority, and the dog immediately trotted to his left side and sat, even though she continued to regard Emily with hostility. "She doesn't like women," he whispered by way of an excuse. "So we won't tell her you're my *w-i-f-e*."

"Does she know she's a *d-o-g?*"

"That's a big *n-o*. Hank tries to tell her from time to time, but she knows better than to listen to him. After all, he's a—"

"—*h-o-r-s-e?*" Emily supplied.

"—horse," Kurt said. "No point in trying to hide it from him. He knows how to spell."

Emily smiled graciously, despite the realization that she'd made a bet with a madman. "I'll just grab my suitcase and go on inside," she said. "While you put my car in the garage and tuck your— friends—into bed."

"Sure thing." He turned the horse toward the barn, the dog at his heels. Then he looked at her. "Oh, Hank stays in the stable, but Melba sleeps with us."

*Us?* Emily blinked and just managed to bite back a scorching denial. He was baiting her, trying to win by simple aggravation, that was all. "Us?" she repeated as calmly as if she were asking him where the sun would come up tomorrow morning. "She sleeps with us?"

He nodded, leaned down to scratch the dog's ear. "I thought I should warn you so you won't be startled."

Scathing words all but burned her tongue, but Emily thought about how much he was going to hate seeing his name embroidered on the butt pocket of all those khaki pants and smiled. "I slept with you, Kurt. After that, I hardly think waking up with a dog would be all that startling."

And on that sweet note, she pulled her suitcase out of the back seat and headed for the house.

# Chapter Six

When Kurt finally came indoors, he found Emily's things in the fourth and spare bedroom. Her clothes hung neatly in the closet, her shoes were paired and positioned across the closet floor, a bottle of nail polish, red, and a handful of Q-Tips, white, sat on the bedside table next to a bookmarked novel. Melba sniffed all around and growled intermittently. "Will you stop that, Mel?" Kurt scolded. "At least wait until I cue you, okay?"

The terrier wagged her tail but kept sniffing. There was something different about the bedroom, Kurt thought. Something besides the obvious factor of Emily's presence. It wasn't perfume, exactly. More of a faint, spicy-sweet fragrance that was hard to pin down and yet was a transient memory in the air. Kurt found it pleasant, despite knowing the elusive scent was going to drive Melba nuts. Which would, in turn, drive Emily crazy. Which would in-

crease the chances of her losing her composure.
Which would get her out of his house all the faster.

Kurt picked up the nail polish and read the color
name off the lid. Red Hot Mama. Somehow he'd
never thought of Emily Dawson as the kind of
woman who would paint her fingernails. Much less
paint them Red Hot Mama red. On the other hand,
he could never have predicted anything she'd done
in the past twenty-four hours. And he'd never have
believed he could be amused by her actions rather
than charging-bull furious. No matter what story she
told—and he'd admit she'd told some pretty good
ones—he knew last night's wedding chapel ceremony, as fake as he still somehow believed it had
been, had everything to do with her ambition to sell
Dawson's Duds in every Western wear market in
the world. Not that he believed his endorsement
would make or break her plans. But she was a determined little thing. Opportunistic and smart, too.
So why hadn't she seen through his bluff about the
car?

He'd expected her to laugh in his face, to tell him
that the car and the endorsement were simply the
price he had to pay for getting dead drunk and being
too stupid to go home before he made a complete
fool of himself. She'd seen an opportunity and
seized it. Much as he might regret his actions, he
didn't fault her for that. But she'd not only accepted
his spur-of-the-moment wager, she anted up every

time he raised the stakes. Get along to win the car? Sure thing. Live together to gain the endorsement bonus? You bet. Stay at his place to accommodate his animals? Well, okay. Share a bed with him and his dog? Considering the way she'd taken over this spare room, probably not.

Kurt was wondering if he should push her on that, hoping to send her screaming down the road, when her legs walked in. Well, actually, all of her walked into the room, but it was her legs that caught him flat-footed and cost him what had been a fairly rational train of thought. She was wearing terry cloth again, only this time it was in the form of a robe. A short robe. Yellow. Or maybe pink. The only thing he was certain of was that she had legs. Really great legs.

"Hello, Kurt," she said evenly, although he could see in her eyes—once he got his testosterone under control and raised his gaze—that he'd startled her. "Hello, d-o-g."

Melba growled but scurried over to get a good long whiff of the newcomer's feet. Kurt was just about to call the terrier to heel when he noticed that Emily's toenails were Red Hot Mama red. Wow, he thought. Who would have believed that Emily—

"You could have left the car keys in another part of the house," she said. "You didn't have to bring them *into* my room."

"Oh," he said, then recovering added, "I came

in to help you move your things into the master bedroom." He held up the bottle of nail polish, as if that clarified his intention. "It's farther down the hall, but don't worry about it. Anyone might have made the same mistake."

"It wasn't a mistake, Kurt. I'm going to be gracious and let Melba have my side of your bed." Emily advanced toward him, and Kurt held his ground, although he did have some trouble breathing. She reached right past him, coming close enough that he forgot about her legs in that spicy-sweet fragrance that suddenly tantalized him, up-close and personal. "No point in upsetting her by exercising my conjugal rights, you know."

Kurt swallowed hard and fought a wave of—attraction? No way. It had to be something else. Nausea, maybe. Or an allergic reaction. Or the casual way she used the word *conjugal*. As if she might slip into bed with him on any given night and—

"Excuse me?" She was looking at him expectantly, and damn it if he didn't start grinning like an idiot before he realized he was blocking her access to the drawer in the bedside table. He stepped aside hastily, and since Melba was on Emily's heels like a vacuum cleaner, Kurt bumped her with his foot. She let out a yelp—although he knew he hadn't injured her—and limped around looking pitiful. That was the trouble with having a beautifully trained dog. Off-camera, she could pick and choose her tricks for their attention value.

"Melba! Heel!" Kurt's voice was sharper than he intended, but he couldn't reward her for acting out her hostilities. "Heel!"

"Oh, poor baby!" Emily's voice crooned to the dog like a lullaby, and before Kurt could stop her, she was kneeling to check the poor baby's paw. And frowning furiously at him, to boot. "You stepped on her," Emily accused.

"I bumped into her. Big difference."

"She's obviously hurt."

"She's not hurt."

"Easy for you to say. You're ten times her size."

"She's trained to limp on command."

"Did you give her the command?"

"No, but—"

"Then, obviously, you stepped on her."

Melba sat, holding up her paw for Emily's soothing pats, looking for all the world like a dog most misunderstood. Kurt frowned at her, but the terrier ignored him and gave Emily's hand a pathetic lick. Little turncoat, he thought. "She's not hurt," he repeated.

Emily ignored him, too, and at the risk of breaking up this tender female-bonding exercise, he called retreat. "If she's still limping tomorrow, I'll take her to the vet." With carefully controlled irritation, Kurt scooped the dog under his arm and headed for the door. "It'll serve her right if he puts her in a full body cast."

"It'll serve you right if he puts you in jail for cruelty to animals."

Kurt stopped, no longer caring how great Emily's legs were. "In two minutes, when she's bouncing around like a puppy, you can apologize for that remark. In the meantime, it might be best if you stayed in your room and—and painted your toenails or something."

"It would be best if *you* stayed out of my room altogether." Annoyance crackled in every nuance of her voice, and if Kurt hadn't been so annoyed himself, he might have suggested she concede the bet right then and go home. "And," she continued, "the next time you want to borrow my nail polish, ask." She held out her hand, and he dropped the bottle into it, considering conceding the bet himself if she'd just go away.

Under his arm, Melba whined softly, and Emily stroked her ear. "If he mistreats you, again, sweetheart, you can come back and sleep with me."

*You do, and I leave everything to Hank in my will,* Kurt told the dog in a glance. Melba looked contrite. Emily smiled, clearly believing she'd won yet another go-round. "If you'll excuse me," she said pleasantly. "I just came in to get my bath gel. I'm on my way to the shower. So, good night."

"Good night," Kurt said tightly, on his way to

turn on the dishwasher, the washing machine and anything else in the house that might use hot water. With any luck at all, she'd freeze before she was half through washing all that hair.

"UP AND AT 'EM! Rise and shine!" A rat-a-tat knock followed the words into the bedroom and startled Emily from a sound sleep. She sat straight up and squinted at Kurt in the doorway. At least she thought it was him standing in the near pitch-dark. "Morning, sunshine." His cheery voice cinched the identification. "Time to look bright-eyed and bushytailed."

Emily dropped back to the mattress with a thud and pulled the covers over her head. "Go away," she mumbled, still chasing sweet slumber.

"Nope. This is a working ranch, and we've got work to do, so prop those brown eyes open and let's get going."

"You go. I'm going back to sleep."

"We go together, sidekick. Remember? Like Batman and Robin? Like Timmy and Lassie?"

"You've mistaken me for Tonto, Lone Ranger. Now go away."

"In your dreams, darlin'. Put those feet on the floor or I'll do it for you."

"Touch my feet and you die a horrible death."

"What's this?" Kurt's voice came closer, dipped in a tease. "Reneging on our bet already? I figured you'd have more sticking power than this, Dawson, but if that's the way you—"

"This has nothing to do with the bet," she said, lowering the covers to her chin. "It has to do with it being the middle of the night."

"It's five, and if you'll recall, we agreed to be together morning, noon and night to keep the wager interesting. I think I was pretty flexible to let you sleep in here last night, but I won't be so understanding this morning."

Emily didn't wake up well at seven, and she hated talking before daybreak. But she'd be damned if she'd let him know she wasn't sharp enough to *understand* him right out of her bedroom. "You have no proof that I ever agreed to anything so preposterous," she said, and pulled the covers over her head.

"You married me, Emily. What could be more preposterous than that?"

He had a point, and she squinted at him over the covers one more time. "Come back at nine and we'll talk about it."

"You meet me at the barn in ten minutes and I'll consider this a near miss. Otherwise, that car is mine, along with all the Dawson's Duds I can wear."

She sat up and eyed him coldly. "Farrah wouldn't have gotten up at this hour, and you wouldn't have made her, either."

"True. But then, she'd have known how to keep me in bed past dawn, too."

Emily scowled, wondering what he'd have to say if she plucked his mustache out hair by hair. "You're a sorry excuse for a husband, McCauley."

"All's fair in wagers and wedlock." He strode to the door, all muscle and male in the morning darkness. "See you in ten minutes…unless you're ready to call off the bet, in which case, I'll be happy to wait until nine to drive you home in my new car."

The pillow was in her hand and then it hit him square on the back of the head. "Sorry," she said. "I meant to throw a brick."

"It's okay." He tossed the pillow back at her. "I meant to marry your sister."

And that, pretty much, woke her up.

FIFTEEN MINUTES later, Emily pushed open the back door and stepped outside, ready to give Kurt the car, the clothes and considerable grief. It had been a stupid bet, anyway. Certainly not worth the aggravation of putting up with him.

On the other hand, it was a beautiful morning. Dawn capped the horizon as softly as a lover's smile, the breezy air smelled fresh and sweetly crisp…and Emily would really hate seeing Kurt drive her car around town. So what if he still loved Carolina? The only thing Emily wanted from him was to win their bet. Oh, yes, and the annulment. If it wasn't Sunday and so early the birds were still yawning, she'd be on the phone with Cousin Milton this very second, demanding he file the papers to-day.

"Grab a hat from inside," Kurt called to her from somewhere near the barn.

Squinting, Emily tried to see him in the dusky light, but the bulky shape of a saddle horse blocked her view. Hat, she thought. He wanted her to bring him a hat. Ducking through the door, she espied a hat rack and a couple of cowboy hats hanging just to the right of the doorway. She chose the grungiest one, twitched it from its hook and let the door slam again behind her. *Some cowboy you are, McCauley,* she chided silently. *Leaving the house without your hat.* She should have made him fetch it himself. She wasn't one of his ranch hands. He couldn't order her around.

With careless alacrity, Emily gave the hat a toss and felt justified when the breeze caught it and floated it back to her hand. For some reason, that made her feel like laughing—and because she normally never felt anything except dead and grouchy at this time of day, she tossed it again. The hat twirled, spun out of reach, and she had to lunge to catch it. The laughter came close to escaping, felt like a promise bubbling inside her, and a quick glance revealed that Kurt was checking the girth of the saddle on a small bay filly and wasn't paying

Emily a bit of attention. So she threw the hat higher, just to see if she could catch it a third time. But the hat sailed up, wobbled, fell and skittered across the ground, kicking up a cloud of dust directly in front of the filly, who sidestepped into Kurt, caught him off balance and sent him sprawling.

*Oops.*

"What the hell are you doing?" He was on his feet in an instant, dusting his chaps and scowling at her. "Put that hat on your head and leave it there."

"My head?" she repeated, belatedly aware that he was wearing a wide-brimmed Stetson. Black—which labeled him a bad guy in her book. "I'm not wearing a hat."

"When you put it on, you will be." He gave the cinch another sharp tug before he gathered the reins and handed them to Emily. "You can't be out all day without a hat."

Emily looked at the saddled horses—the small filly and the lanky roan—then at Kurt. "You woke me up at the crack of dawn to put me on a horse?"

"I didn't think you'd want to walk."

"Well, that doesn't mean I want to *ride,* either."

He swung astride the roan. "Say the word, Emily, and you're free to go home and do whatever the hell you want to."

"You are so delusional, McCauley." She attempted a fierce frown and wound up with a long sigh. "As if I could remember the word at this ungodly hour."

He grinned, and Emily's knees went Jell-O. It was grossly unfair that the man could look so manly, so appealing, so—okay, she'd admit it—*attractive* this early in the morning. Doubly unfair that he could do it while wearing a black hat. "Sling your leg over Suzy, there," he said, "and I'll take you out for breakfast."

*Breakfast?* She eyed the filly with new incentive. "What did you call her?"

"Suzy." He turned the roan in a tight circle. "This is Joe."

"Why aren't you riding Hank?"

"It's his day off."

Emily arched a skeptical brow, and Kurt shrugged. "Hank is a valuable commodity, and the insurance company sort of frowns on using him for ordinary ranch work. So days like today, I ride one of the ordinary horses, like Joe, here."

"You don't have to take that kind of insult, Joe," Emily advised the roan. "Buck him off. Show him you're no *ordinary* horse."

Joe swished his tail and restlessly stamped a foot but made no other move to be extraordinary. Kurt patted the horse's neck. "Get in the saddle," he told Emily. "Before Suzy loses her patience."

"Hello, Suzy." Emily rubbed the bay's nose before she moved to the horse's left, positioned the reins and lifted herself into the saddle. "Horses should have horse names," she argued, just to see what she could get started. "Not human names."

He looked at her. "If it will improve your attitude, today we'll call this one Race and that one you're on Plow. Now, put that hat on and let's get moving. We've got work to do."

"What about breakfast?"

"In due time, morning glory. In due time." He flicked the reins and the roan took off at a brisk trot.

Suzy didn't need any encouragement to follow, and Emily dug in her knees to keep from being bounced off. She slapped the grungy hat onto her head where it promptly settled halfway down the bridge of her nose, all but blocking her vision. Great, she thought. Super. Up at dawn. Straddling a horse before the sun crested the morning. A hat—too big for her head—that, despite its dingy white color, did not make her feel like one of the good guys. And nothing ahead of her but a view of cowboy butt.

On the other hand...it was a beautiful morning.

Thirty minutes later, Emily was sitting in the breezy kitchen of Ray and Josie Scott, surrounded by delicious smells and easy conversation. Ray was the ranch foreman, and he and Josie had lived two miles back from the main house for most of Kurt's life. Their original trailer had grown room by added-on room into a sprawling rectangle of a house, with a porch that wrapped around three sides and a redwood deck across the back. Kurt joined them for Sunday breakfast whenever he was at the ranch, and Josie spoiled him like the son she and Ray had never been blessed to have. Most everyone in Fortune City knew Ray was worth his weight in gold as a foreman and could have moved on anytime he wanted. But he'd stuck by the McCauleys through thick and thin and now was obviously taking great satisfaction in Kurt's success. It was Josie, though, who was treated to Kurt's enthusiastic and affectionate hug, and in that one gesture, Emily saw that he was as vulnerable to tender loving care as anyone else.

While Josie sliced ham and potatoes for frying, Kurt pummeled bread dough into rough lumps that, once baked, fluffed up into feathery-light biscuits. Emily sat at the table with a cup of coffee and with Ray, who was momentarily engrossed in the stock sale flyers, and listened as Kurt and Josie discussed a mystery novel, a newly released movie and an article on liposuction in *Cosmopolitan*. Emily was pretty certain that he didn't read women's magazines as a matter of course, and the idea that he'd do so just to have something to talk about with Josie impressed her.

It impressed her a lot…but not nearly as much as the fact that he did the dishes.

"It's hot, McCauley," she told him around eleven.

"Nah," he said, although she was right.

"These fences are in great shape, as far as I can see."

"Next section may be in pieces. Next range gate may be open," he said, although he knew for a fact it wasn't. "Tedious work, riding fences, but it's got to be done."

"And you're certain I couldn't just ride on back to the house and wait for you? Or I could go back and stay with Josie."

"Not if you want to adhere to the terms of our bet. Morning, noon and—"

"—night. I remember. But this is such a waste of time. I could be taking a nap."

"You could be mucking out stalls, too. I'm no happier about this than you are, Emily." The truth was, he wasn't all that unhappy to have her company. Oh, sure, she'd grumbled from time to time, yawned a lot, complained about being rousted from bed by a sadistic, evil lunatic. But in between attempts to aggravate him, she brought him up to date on subjects near and dear to the residents of Fortune City. From who won the regional barrel-racing competition to why old Dr. Stanley was sporting a black eye, she told him the gossip and filled him in on the events he'd missed. They talked about her store and her plans for it. She asked about Hank and Melba and the methods he'd used to train them. He told her as many animal anecdotes as he could easily recall and even a few he invented on the spot, just to see if he could get her to laugh.

Emily laughed easily, he discovered. Without hesitation or self-consciousness. A friendly laugh that never failed to perk up the ears of the horses and seemed to put new energy in their steps. A laugh a man could get accustomed to hearing. The kind of laugh a man could get lost in—if he didn't have any better sense.

A few times Kurt found himself watching her mouth, waiting to catch the beginning of laughter…or her smile. She had a great smile, too. Warm, wide, soft as a feather, lighting where it would, lingering whimsically on the fringes of their conversation. It took him the better part of the morning to figure out it was her smile that kept capturing his attention and the rest of the day to wonder why he'd never noticed it before. Not exactly the kind of thing a guy really pondered, just something he was smart enough to enjoy.

So they rode a fool's errand and talked. They stopped to rest the horses and talked. Emily offered her opinion on subjects as wide-ranging as movies and pickles. Kurt teased her about her gawky adolescence and the trophy she'd once won for bareback donkey riding. He missed no opportunity to mention the bet and the myriad reasons she couldn't possibly win. She countered with all the reasons he was an idiot to think he could best her in any contest of wills.

Carolina was the one topic they both avoided. Emily, for reasons known only to her. Kurt, because he didn't care to know the specifics of the whirlwind courtship, the fast and fancy wedding.

Truth be told, he was much more interested in his own wedding. Friday was still a big blur, and yesterday he hadn't exactly been at his best. But there were details he felt he ought to know, even if he couldn't quite bring himself to ask.

In fact, that was the main reason he and Emily were out here now—because he couldn't remember much about getting married and he'd be damned if he was going to admit that to the general population of Fortune City. Or at least to those souls brave enough to call or show up at his house today and ask. Kurt knew he'd have to face the questions sooner or later, understood that the consequences of his stupidity were already nipping at his heels. He just didn't see any pressing need to deal with the complications today. So he'd blackmailed Emily into this escape to the wide-open spaces. And they weren't going back until long after visiting hours.

Or until she gave up on winning the bet, whichever came first.

EMILY RECOGNIZED busywork when she saw it, and riding the long miles of fence on Kurt's property fit the description to a T. She knew as well as anyone else in town that Kurt employed his share of ranch hands and had long ago hired a competent foreman. She'd even sold Ray his last pair of boots—tan snakeskin with a leather diamond inset—crafted by a Native American artist whose finely made footwear was better than anything else on the market. In Emily's opinion, anyway. She planned to feature the entire line of boots in the first Dawson's Duds catalog, along with the McCauley's Khakis and several other name-brand items available at her store. Her business plan was coming along quite nicely, and now that Kurt's endorsement was hers for the taking, she was thinking about revising the initial printing on the catalog upward to a nicer, rounder number.

Of course, today had proved that Kurt was going to make her earn every letter of that endorsement. Even now, relaxing in a hot bath, every muscle in her body protested the long hours in the saddle. But she'd stuck it out. She and Suzy had kept pace. Emily had been pleasant, upbeat, full of conversation. In fact, she'd done her utmost to wear Kurt out with her chatter.

But much to her wonderment, he'd been pleasant, too. More than pleasant, really. Thoughtful. Considerate. Even—surprise—entertaining. For the first time, Emily realized that Kurt was—even bigger surprise—interesting. Despite the fact that he'd

seized every chance to goad her into losing her cool
and consequently the bet, for the most part their conversation flowed naturally, sometimes focusing on
him, sometimes on her. He'd even made her laugh
a few times—would wonders never cease? But all
in all, the day had flown by in a haze of fence posts,
rest stops, riding and—biggest surprise of all—good
company.

Emily was even feeling a tad guilty about taking
the car, the endorsement and a whopping amount of
his pride. Not that she wasn't fully aware he had
ulterior motives, too. But she was going to win—it
was becoming a matter of principle—and it was kind
of nice to know that when she drove away in the
Mustang with Kurt's signed endorsement in her
pocket, she could truthfully say her two weeks with
him hadn't been the nightmare she'd expected. She
might even go so far as to have a fantasy or two
about him.

"Emily?" He thumped on the door in a bone-
jarring boom, boom, boom. "I'm moving your
things into my room tonight—unless you're ready
to admit you're in over your head with this wager."

On second thought, any fantasy she entertained
about Kurt McCauley was going to involve murder.

"HAS IT OCCURRED to you that sleeping together
might negate our claim to an annulment?" She
stood in the doorway of his bedroom, barefoot and

still dripping, wrapped in her terry-cloth robe, hair wet as seaweed and just about as attractive, determined to set this man straight on where she was—and wasn't—spending the night.

He looked at her, his gaze lingering quite obviously on her legs. "Nope."

"Even living under the same roof like this might have a negative bearing on the annulment," she said, striving for a reasonable tone to combat his mule-headed persistence. "Until I've had a chance to discuss the matter with Milton, I think we should—at the very least—behave circumspectly."

"Circumspectly," he repeated, rolling the syllables on his tongue, making her feel like she was butting her head against a wall. "That would mean living under the same roof but being careful not to let anyone think we're sleeping in the same bed?" His smile curved slowly. "A little late for that, isn't it? You may want other people to believe this is simply a platonic marriage, but the truth is we had a wedding night. Or did you forget, darlin'?"

Emily gulped. Okay, so she always got caught in her lies. That didn't mean she couldn't be honest now. "I just made that up," she said.

"Uh-huh. You don't have to spare my feelings, Emily. I know it wasn't great for you, but I'll make it up to you. Tonight, if you want."

Oh, he was good. Pretending he didn't know as well as she did that nothing had happened that night, no matter what she'd told him. But if this was his best attempt to corral her into a retreat, he was a dozen fence posts short of accomplishing the job. "I'm not sleeping with you, Kurtis," she said firmly. "Get over it."

"Then I win the bet."

"In a pig's eye." She flicked a water droplet off her shoulder. "The bet is that I can get along with you for two weeks, which I am going to do no matter how difficult you try to make it by bringing up this stupid idea of sharing a bed."

He almost gave himself away—she saw the tug of humor in the slight twitch of his lips—but he caught himself and produced a what-did-I-say? expression. "I'm only trying to sleep with my wife. Which is, I might add, a perfectly normal activity for newlyweds."

"We may be married, McCauley, but we are not newlyweds. This is harassment, plain and simple, and you ought to be ashamed of yourself for stooping to such shenanigans."

He stacked all the things he'd carried from her room on his dresser. After lining up the nail polish, Q-Tips and a wooden back scratcher—Lord only knew where he'd picked that up—he turned to her with a pseudofrown. "I'm merely trying to insure that we both abide by the rules of our little wager, Emily. That's all."

"Really?" she said, knowing exactly what he was

trying to insure. "I thought you were pulling every underhanded trick in the book to romance that car right out from under me."

He smiled. "That, too."

"Well, all I can say is you should have read the fine print, because I am not going to get into any bed that has you in it."

"I could sweep you off your feet again."

"I don't think so."

"I did it once," he argued. "I could do it again."

"I told you I made that up."

"You don't believe I could romance you back into my bed, do you, Emily?"

She knew in her bones this was a setup, had been from the moment he'd pounded on the bathroom door, but still she heard herself rise to the bait. "You couldn't romance me with all the roses, all the champagne, all the violins *and* every diamond in the universe," she told him flatly.

"That's not the kind of romance I had in mind." He smiled and came closer. Much too close. "I was thinking of something more…personal."

"Try offering me a car."

"What I'm offering is better…much better." His gaze dropped to her lips with a sure intent, and he stepped even closer. Into her space. Uncomfortably, intriguingly inside her space.

Emily wished she could laugh right in his face, but her knees were doing that Jell-O thing again, and it was all she could do to hold her ground. "You know, McCauley, until about ten minutes ago I was beginning to think you weren't such a bad guy, after all. Then you have to go and behave like some two-bit Lothario who's pining for a stupid kiss."

He shook his head as if her words had stung him. Which, of course, was impossible, considering his hide was as thick as any elephant's. "Emily, Emily, Emily," he said sadly. "What's a little kiss between husband and wife?"

"Blackmail?" she suggested tightly, the freshly showered scent of him all but filling her up by sheer osmosis.

He smiled, so sure of himself that if she could have lifted her foot without falling over, she'd have kicked him in the shin. "'The lady doth protest too much, methinks.'"

Shakespeare. Sheesh. Did the man have no shame? "Look, Romeo, let me make something perfectly clear. This little scam of yours is not going to fly with me. I'm going to win this wager, come hell or heaven, and there is nothing—*nothing*—you can do to scare me off. Understand?"

His breath was warm, moist, close to her face, and she knew without a shadow of a doubt that if he had the audacity to kiss her right here and right now, she'd…she'd kiss him back. Which was a bad idea. A really bad idea. Even if it suddenly seemed like a good idea. A *really* good idea.

"Well, Emily," he said in a voice as silky and soft as a con man's. "You can't fault a guy for trying, now, can you?" He bent closer still, taking up more of her space, more energy, more…air.

And then he took her lips in a soft, exploratory kiss—that blazed through Emily like a fire and all but barbequed the Red Hot Mama polish on every one of her ten toes.

"Now you've done it," Emily said in a voice that tried hard to sound offended, but managed to be merely breathless. "Now you've really done it."

For once, Kurt was in complete agreement. He'd meant to kiss her sassy mouth and scare the living daylights out of her…although exactly why he'd thought a kiss would do that eluded him at the moment. Certainly he'd meant to convince her that he wasn't kidding, that she was going to have to share his bed in order to win the bet. Not that he'd had the least intention of sleeping with her, of course. He'd just thought insisting would make her so mad she'd lose her temper and at the very least slug him good and hard, which would have cost her the car and everything else.

But kissing Emily wasn't what he'd expected. Oh, no, he'd expected her to respond like an amateur, with closed mouth, closed eyes and closed mind. He didn't know about her eyes, but her mouth and her mind had definitely been open. Kurt couldn't remember the last time a woman had returned his kiss with such warmth and passion, such a healthy enthusiasm. And being a red-blooded, all-American cowboy, he'd been easily duped into meeting that enthusiasm halfway. Hell, if he'd been any more enthusiastic, they'd be in bed together right now. And that really would have tied this situation into a hangman's noose.

As it was, that single, sensual kiss had added a whole new set of knots. Until a few seconds ago, he could handle the idea that he might, in reality, be legally married to Emily. He could share his mornings, noons and nights with her because he knew that she knew there was nothing between them but a friendly animosity.

Except now they'd done it. He'd gone and kissed her, she'd gone and kissed him back and now *he* knew that *she* knew there was something else…a raw and rowdy physical attraction. And that awareness changed everything. Because now, neither one of them could call a halt to this foolishness without tacitly admitting to the other that there was a powerful attraction at work and that they'd rather call off the bet than face the daily temptation of it.

Emily still stood in front of him, still damp and sweet-smelling from her bath, her hair in wet strings about her shoulders, her legs stretching a ridiculously long length below the yellow terry-cloth robe. She was also furious. It took a moment for the anger to push aside the dazed and bemused expression on her face, but it arrived. "You are an idiot, McCauley, if you think that kissing me changed anything. That car, and your name, are mine. Get used to it." She took an unsteady step toward the door. "Now I'm going to my bed and I suggest you get into yours, because tomorrow we're riding *my* fences. Bring the car around at eight. And wear something besides jeans. Tomorrow, cowboy, you're going to meet the world of marketing."

Kurt wanted to argue. He really did. But when he looked at her all he could think about was kissing her again. Which wouldn't be a good idea. Not a good idea at all.

"One more thing," she said pausing on the other side—the safer side—of his bedroom doorway. "From now on, there'll be no more mention of sharing a bed. Otherwise, I'm instructing Cousin Milton to forget the annulment and start dividing the property."

Okay, so some response was in order, but he'd be damned if he could think of anything except the way her lips had all but melted into his and how much he'd like to feel them do it again.

"Good night, Kurtis," Emily said. "I will *see* you in the *morning*."

*Lucky you,* he thought as he watched her beat a fairly dignified retreat. He had a feeling that when sleep finally came to him, he'd be seeing her all night in his dreams.

"Well, it's just you and me tonight, Melba," he said in a voice designed to follow Emily down the hall. But to his consternation, Melba jumped from the bed and trotted after Emily without so much as a fare-thee-well.

*Females,* Kurt thought, and slammed his door.

# Chapter Seven

Kurt brought the car around promptly at eight, as directed. He wore his least faded pair of Wranglers, a freshly ironed shirt and his best hat, figuring that was as far as he wanted to go in following Emily's instructions. He'd slept well, despite his prediction that he wouldn't, and he'd dreamed about kissing Carolina. Well, he'd started out kissing her, at any rate, even though by the end of the dream it was Emily's lips on the other side of his.

Of course, it was only a dream. The fact that he even remembered who he'd been kissing in it was probably a fluke. As to the unforgettable fact that he had, indeed, kissed Emily last night? Well, he'd taken his share of psychology classes and figured his feelings for Carolina were mixed-up in that kiss somehow, too. There was a certain similarity in their appearance. Emily had better legs, that was for certain, and he couldn't quite remember the color of Carolina's eyes. Nine chances out of ten, they were brown like Emily's, but he couldn't say for sure one way or the other. As for his reaction to kissing Emily—well, hell, he was a male, and any kissin' was good. Plus it had been a while since he'd set lips on Carolina.

Something told him he would've remembered a kiss as warm and passionate as the one he and Emily had shared. Hell, he knew in his gut that if Carolina had ever once kissed him with that much enthusiasm, he wouldn't have been able to leave her behind, much less stay away long enough for her to meet and marry someone else. Still, he didn't see any other explanation for it. He'd reacted to kissing Emily because she reminded him of his lost love. That had to be the way of it. Otherwise, if he hadn't somehow transferred his feelings for Carolina, however briefly, to Emily, he just might find himself in a real hot kettle of stew.

"Good morning." Emily got into the car, startling him from his thoughts and looking like a million bucks. Her hair was tied at her nape with a yellow bow, and the morning sun set the highlights in her hair on fire. Her long skirt was a mass of bright colors and intentional wrinkles, topped with a soft-looking red cotton sweater belted with a high-dollar silver chain. She wore a silver necklace and earrings, and she was definitely the prettiest thing he'd seen this early in the morning for months. Except, perhaps, for yesterday, when she'd looked grumpy, but still pretty. "You look nice," he said, even though that was a considerable understatement.

She eyed him skeptically. "Thanks. So do you."

"I'd have worn my McCauley khakis if you'd ever given me a pair."

"They're not for sale yet," she said confidently. "But as soon as your name is stitched on the pockets, I'll be sure you get to buy the first pair."

"Counting your chickens before they're hatched, aren't you?"

"Oh, I don't think so. They're incubating quite nicely, and I have no doubt at all that McCauley khakis will hit the market within the next three or four months. I'm even willing to bet on it."

He frowned at her, at her perky bow, her perky attitude and her perky...lips. Then, eyes front, he put the car in gear and roared down the drive at a fast, dust-stirring clip, noting with pleasure that she had to reach back and hold onto her hair bow.

"How DO YOU want to handle this?" he asked as they pulled into the parking lot of Dawson's Duds.

She let go of what remained of the ponytail, revealing a yellow bow that was squashed and unperky, and tried to smooth the wild strands of her hair into order. "How do I want to handle this?" she repeated. "Today, you mean?"

He nodded.

"Well, I'm going to tell you what to do and then

I want you to do it. That won't be too difficult for you, will it?''

He managed a smile, knowing he hadn't had enough coffee yet to wrangle with her. ''I meant, how do you want to handle the questions. You know as well as I do that any time anyone walks through the front door of your store today, they're going to be looking for something more than new duds.''

The thought had obviously occurred to her, too, because her lips tightened and frown lines creased her forehead. ''Why should we have to explain anything? It's not like it's anyone else's business.''

He raised an eyebrow. ''Fortune City may not be the smallest town in Nevada, Emily, but you couldn't tell that from the grapevine around here.''

She sighed, admitting the truth of that. ''What do you think we should tell them?''

''I asked you first.''

''Well, I don't know. The truth, I guess. It's not as if we have anything to hide.''

Kurt barely managed to bite back a grin at that naive statement. ''You know, you're right. We're just two people who've never liked each other much who suddenly got married, won a classic car and made a bet that they could live together for two weeks without one committing some heinous crime against the other. Can't imagine why anyone would be curious about that.''

Her shoulders sagged. "No one is going to believe us."

"Which brings me back to my original question—how do you want to handle this?"

She considered, her teeth scraping her bottom lip with worry. "I don't see any reason to lie," she said finally. "We'll just answer any questions as truthfully as possible and try not to say any more than is absolutely necessary. Think that will work?"

*Not in a million years.* "I suppose it's worth a try," he said with a shrug, suddenly glad she'd insisted he come to work with her today. Considering the whoppers she'd told him regarding their love-match marriage and the most-romantic-night-of-her-life wedding night, he figured the truth might just turn out to be pretty damn entertaining.

RENETTA HAD WORKED for Emily for nearly eighteen months and had never once driven into the telephone pole behind the store. But she pulled into the parking lot just as Kurt held open the back door for Emily, and, staring openmouthed at the two of them as she drove past, Renetta did it. She drove smack into the pole.

Her slick little Dodge Dakota made a decisive whomp and bounced back, front fender crumpled like a piece of tin foil. The telephone pole shivered for a full minute, and by the time it stopped, Emily and Kurt had both reached the truck to render aid to the driver. But Renetta sat, unhurt, behind the wheel, looking wide-eyed from one face to the other. "Lord love a ladybug, Emily, you *did* it! You *slept* with him, didn't you?" Renetta blurted out the incriminating words in the aftershock of hitting the pole and was obviously, instantly, excruciatingly embarrassed.

The sixty-four-thousand-dollar question that was on everyone's mind, including Kurt's, had been asked for the first time.

But not for the last.

"DON'T answer that phone," Emily directed.

They were inside her small office—Renetta, Kurt and Emily—and the hands of the clock were edging toward nine. If Emily had thought this through, she'd have insisted Kurt stay at the ranch instead of coming with her. Of course, if she'd thought *anything* through, she wouldn't have gone to the bar Friday night, wouldn't have gone to Las Vegas, wouldn't have married him, would *not* have agreed to this silly bet. If being with him morning, noon and night didn't do her in, her friends definitely would.

"Are you sure?" Renetta asked timidly. "It could be a supplier."

"A supplier would hang up after the first twenty rings," Emily said, knowing she sounded snippish, knowing her short temper had something to do with

Kurt and everything to do with last night's kiss. It probably had a lot to do with the way he leaned against the wall, too, and had his arms crossed, and wore his hat pulled low, and the snug fit of his jeans and the way he tried to hide his grin below that overthick mustache. Plus, she could see the amusement sparkling in his blue eyes like a villain's dastardly smile. Oh, she would get him for this—just as soon as she figured out exactly what it was he was doing that annoyed her so much.

"No one comes in and no calls get answered before the store opens," she said firmly, although in five minutes there would be no such thing as a private moment. Normally, she and Renetta had a pretty good system for managing both the office and the retail sales, but today wasn't going to be any ordinary day. It was going to be busy. Very busy. Emily knew she should have called in her two part-time employees, but that would mean she and Renetta would be filling the evening shift, too. Better to tough it out. One thing was certain, though. Kurt was due a full day of backbreaking busywork, preferably in the back and out of sight. Maybe gagged, too. "Come on, Kurt," she said. "Let me introduce you to the stockroom and your first assignment."

"Guess I'd better start getting acquainted with the business end of this place." Kurt winked at Renetta, who blushed anew. Then he pushed lazily away from the wall and looked at Emily. "Lead the way, darlin'."

Emily thought about leading with a right hook but didn't want him to think she couldn't get along. "The stockroom's back here," she called when she realized he wasn't behind her but had walked toward the front of the store. "Kurt? Back here."

"There must be a dozen people out there, already," he said, shaking his head. "What kind of sale are you having?"

"A busybody sale—and you're the main busybody." Emily slipped behind him, grabbed his arm and gave it a tug. "Would you stop staring at the customers? Come on."

"I hate to contradict you, darlin', but they're staring at me."

"No, they're not." She tugged again, wanting to get him into the back before the entire crowd spotted him.

"Well, they're staring at the two of us, then." He looked at her, catching her unaware, jarring loose her libido with a flash of his infamous smile. "What say we give them something to talk about?"

"Are you insane? We're the main topic of conversation already."

"Oh, come on, Emily. Where's your sense of the ridiculous? Plant one on me here in full view of the day's first customers."

"K-kiss you?" she said with a slight stutter. Just

the word sent a fiery heat searing right through her. "I don't th-think so."

His smile deepened, angling into a crooked charm. "*Kiss?* Who said anything about kissing? I thought maybe you'd pop me a good one. A black eye could really set tongues awaggin'."

She let go of his arm, although she would have loved to give it a good, sound pinch. "Come with me, you moron, and if you will just stay out of the way today, I'll handle this."

He followed her to the back. "So, you want me to be the strong, silent type, huh?"

"I want you to act like a rock and drown." She entered the stockroom and flipped on the light. "And if anyone corners you back here, remember, we agreed to simply tell the truth. With as few details as possible. Got it?"

"You can count on me," he said.

GENNA and Mary Lynn were the first customers to set foot inside the store once Emily unlocked the doors. Calling them *customers* was something of a stretch, though, considering the only thing the two women were in the market for was gossip.

"Give it up, girl," Mary Lynn said, clamping a hand on Emily's elbow. "We want the whole story and we want it now."

"Yes." Genna grabbed the other arm. "You

didn't call. You didn't write. What have you been *doing* the last forty-eight hours?''

Emily nodded to the curiosity seekers filing into the store and sent them a telepathic message—Buy, buy, buy. ''Not much,'' she said. ''What have you two been doing?''

Genna gave her a meaningful look. ''Tell us *everything* before we plain *die* from speculating about it.''

''Genna filled me in on the wedding.'' Mary Lynn squeezed Emily's captive arm. ''I cannot *believe* I missed that! If I'd thought for one second *you* were going to marry him, a Texas twister couldn't have kept me from being there.''

''You didn't miss much,'' Emily said in a breezy tone, although she didn't feel breezy in the slightest.

''Only the event of the century.'' Mary Lynn rolled her eyes. ''You know there's a rumor floating around that you drugged him.''

''There's also a rumor involving a shotgun and a pair of roller skates.'' Genna frowned fiercely at Mary Lynn. ''But what we *really* want to know is where you were all weekend. We called. We left messages. We drove by your house. It's as if you just *disappeared* after we dropped you and Kurt off at the hotel. So what in the heck have you been doing?''

Emily darted a glance to the register, which Renetta had had to abandon in response to a request for assistance. "Riding fences."

"*Ooh*, riding *fences*." Mary Lynn gave an unladylike guffaw. "Like we're going to believe *that*? Come on, Emily, we're your *friends*."

Okay, so the truth wasn't what they wanted to hear. Emily edged toward the register, dragging them with her, wondering what she'd have to tell them before they'd go away. "You guys didn't come in here expecting me to say that Kurt and I spent the whole weekend in bed together, did you?"

"Yes!" Mary Lynn's eyes widened with tawdry interest as her voice nearly exploded with excitement. "Yes! You did it? You actually *slept* with Kurt McCauley?"

Every eye of every eavesdropper in the place swung toward Emily, who decided if life's embarrassing moments were going to gang up on her like this, she wasn't going down without a fight. "I can't tell you *that*, Mary Lynn." Smiling bravely, she slipped from their grasp and ducked behind the checkout counter. "You'll have to read about it in the *National Inquirer*. Kurt and I are giving them an *exclusive* interview."

"That's right," Kurt said, coming up suddenly behind Emily and slipping his arm possessively around her shoulders. "We're committed to telling the *truth*, aren't we, darlin'?"

Emily's head swiveled toward him, and she got

caught in his evil grin. It was, she thought, too damn bad that she hadn't given him that black eye when she had the chance. "Finished steaming out those wrinkles already?" she asked, referring to his assigned task of unpacking several boxes of new garments and getting them ready to hang. "I thought you'd be in the stockroom for hours."

"Heard the bell and figured you and Renetta could use a little help out here." His smile swept from Genna to Mary Lynn. "Could I interest either of you ladies in a new pair of boots?"

"Honey, you could sell me a bulldogger at a rodeo." Mary Lynn leaned confidingly against the register counter. "Got anything in my size?"

Genna laughed, and Emily took the opportunity to shrug off Kurt's arm...except he didn't seem to want to be shrugged. This was probably his idea of helping. "Hello, Kurt," Genna said. "How's the blushing bridegroom?"

His smile didn't miss a beat. "Tired," he answered. "Emily and I have been riding fences."

"Riding fences," Genna repeated in an I-wasn't-born-yesterday tone of voice. "Really."

"And that's the reason you're tired?" Mary Lynn gave her best give-me-the-real-story impersonation of Barbara Walters. "Riding *fences?*"

Kurt nodded. "Plus I didn't get much sleep the last couple of nights."

Mary Lynn grinned like the Cheshire cat. "Now,

who would have thought our considerate little Emily would keep a man *up* all night?"

Emily nearly choked and made a second attempt to dislodge Kurt's protective arm without drawing undue attention to her efforts. "Don't you two have to be at work about now?" she asked the women pointedly. "The bank does still open at nine, doesn't it?"

"I called and said we'd be late," Mary Lynn explained with obvious delight. "Sam Baxter's a vice president now, you know, and he told me to take as much time as needed to get a full report. He says he thinks he was the flower girl at your wedding, but he can't remember for sure."

"Kipp was the flower girl," Kurt said amiably. "Nellis was best man, and Sam escorted the bride down the aisle."

"That is *not* what happened," Emily said, wondering why Kurt couldn't have just stayed in the back room. She also didn't understand how he could be in such a good mood, or look so relaxed and rested. No matter what he claimed about a sleep deficit, he obviously hadn't been troubled all night by ridiculous dreams about... Well, never mind what they'd been about. She was determined to forget last night in its sordid entirety. "Tell them the truth, Kurt."

"The truth is Elvis could have been the flower girl for all I remember about the wedding," he said, still smiling, still squeezing her shoulder like he had some right to do so. "It isn't until *after* the ceremony that—" here he paused to let his smile slide to Emily "—my memory clicks in." He made it sound like he'd done something besides snore.

"Sam and Max weren't even inside the chapel," Emily said, because it seemed important to clarify something. "They were outside, I think."

Genna gladly supplied the missing detail. "They were outside, holding Farrah down so she couldn't bust up the wedding. Man, was she *hot!* You should see the bruise on Max's shin."

"Genna," Emily said. "I'm sure no one wants to talk about this."

"Are you kidding? The whole town is buzzing with it." Genna's red-gold curls bobbed excitedly. "Jeannie even told me she heard that someone called Carolina on her honeymoon to find out if the rumors were true."

"Word is," Mary Lynn added with a significant eyebrow wiggle, "Carolina's fit to be tied."

Kurt cleared his throat, and although his smile didn't fade, he did drop his arm from around Emily. "I can't imagine Carolina would be all that interested."

Genna and Mary Lynn exchanged an arch look before they turned to Emily. "He doesn't really know Carolina very well anymore, does he?"

And he wasn't likely to get reacquainted, either,

Emily thought. Not now, anyway. But she didn't see any point in talking about her sister. That was definitely not going to help this situation. Getting these loudmouths out of her store would help. It would help a lot. But just as she opened her mouth to suggest that her friends hit the road, the door chimed and in walked Nellis, Kipp and Jeannie. Did no one in this whole town have to report to work on time?

"Hello, newlyweds," Kipp called with a knowing smirk.

Nellis snickered.

"Hello, yourself," Kurt said...and then the game of twenty questions, minus nineteen, began all over again.

KURT SET a perspiring can of soda and a take-out sack on Emily's desk before he slumped into the chair across from her, propped his boots on one corner of the desk and popped the top of his drink. "It's late," he said. "But it's lunch."

Emily glanced at the clock. "Two-thirty, and not a single customer in the store. For the first time since I opened Dawson's Duds, I can honestly say I am relieved not to be ringing up a sale." She lifted the soda can in mute testimony to the crazy morning. "Thanks. This dose of caffeine may just get me through the rest of the day."

He gestured at the sack. "The sandwich would probably do you more good."

"I'm not very hungry, but thanks, anyway."

"You feel okay?"

"Other than this sick feeling in the pit of my stomach? Yes." She tipped the soda can to her lips and sipped. "Do you think there was even one person in this town who missed coming in today?"

"I didn't see your parents."

"Dad called," she said with a sigh. "Remember that message about how they wanted me to come for supper one night this week? Well, it's now a command performance. Tonight."

"Couldn't you say we have other plans? We could tell them we have to drive back to Vegas and pick up your van."

"Already taken care of." She began tracing her initials into the condensation on the can. "Renetta's brother and his friend went to retrieve it this afternoon. It'll probably be parked out back by the time we leave. Don't worry about my folks. The marching orders don't include you."

The soda can paused partway to his mouth. "I wasn't invited?"

"I told Dad you wouldn't be there." She managed a weary smile. "Don't worry, Kurt. I can handle them. This doesn't involve you."

"How do you figure?" He rested the soda on the chair arm. "Are you more married than I am?"

"No, but—"

"No ifs, ands or buts," he stated. "I am involved,

Emily, and I'm going with you to explain to your parents. End of discussion.''

She lifted an eyebrow. ''You're being kind of bossy this afternoon.''

''I'm considering a new career in sales. You did note that I sold more merchandise today than you and Renetta put together, didn't you?''

''Forget bossy. You're just flat-out cocky.''

He grinned. ''Go ahead, insult me. You're not getting out of paying me a commission.''

''I ought to charge you double for all the mischief you made today.''

''Me?'' He tried to look innocent, which was impossible, futile and sort of funny. ''I was on my best behavior, talking to the customers, following orders, helping out.''

''Whoa there, mister. Back up to that talking to the customers part. Admit it, McCauley, you took great pains to foster more speculation about our relationship than you put to rest.''

''I told the truth and nothing but the truth.'' He paused, pursed his lips in consideration. ''Well, okay, maybe that part about the flower girl wasn't, but the rest of it was absolutely true. To the best of my knowledge.''

''Uh-huh. I'm fast discovering there's always a loophole with you, Kurt. I was standing right there when you told Nellis and Kipp that our hotel room offered every amenity.''

"Every amenity a man could desire, I believe is the way I phrased it," he admitted serenely. "And it did. That is the truth, now, Emily, isn't it?"

"Yes, and they went away thinking *I* offered a few of those amenities myself."

His smile broadened. "Well, you did, didn't you?"

It was ridiculous, really, but his teasing sent a heated blush rising to the roots of her hair. "I told you, I made that up."

"But we both know you only said that to protect my feelings." The laughter in his eyes told her the shoe was now on the other foot, and he wasn't going to let her off the hook so easily. "I'm still willing to make our wedding night up to you, Em. Just say the word. Anytime. Anywhere."

She took a slug of cola to cool off her hot thoughts and wiped her mouth. "Did you have to tell poor Mrs. Entermyer you were so bleary-eyed happy at the sight of me walking down the aisle that you nearly passed out at the altar?"

"The woman asked me straight out if I knew how lucky I was that a decent woman would agree to marry me. Not much answer a man can make to a statement like that."

"You might have tried a simple yes."

"I did tell her you won me in a cowboy raffle. That should set her to wondering what kind of decent woman you really are."

"Or how hard I had to wrestle to get you to that wedding chapel." Emily smiled. "Mrs. Entermyer doesn't hear too well."

"Either way, I'd wager that she'll be wondering about us for some time to come."

"Which brings us back to my point about your making your own brand of mischief. We should not be enjoying anything about this nutty marriage."

"Speak for yourself. I'm enjoying the heck out of not being married to Farrah Phillips."

"That's not what you said yesterday."

"You never said I had to tell the truth about everything." He put his feet on the floor and leaned forward, his expression sincere. For once. "This is a nutty situation, Emily. I don't deny that it's mostly my fault and that it never should have happened. But hell, I can't go around regretting every stupid thing I've ever done. That's all I'd find time to do. I mean, what's the worst that can happen? The annulment takes longer than a couple of weeks? People in this one-horse town don't have any more weighty issues to ponder than if you and I slept together? Somebody takes away our birthdays?" He shook his head. "Believe me, darlin', we could have a lot bigger worries than being married to each other for a few weeks."

Emily sighed and set her cola aside. "I suppose you're right, Kurt. But I have a great deal of respect for marriage, and I'm ashamed of myself for entering into this one with such—such... Oh, I don't know. Disregard, I guess." She was horrified to feel a sudden, hot rush of tears and tried furiously to blink them back. "I'm sorry," she murmured, feeling three days worth of circumstances pushing for release. "I don't know what's wrong with me today."

Emily sensed his hesitation, but still he was on his feet and around the desk before the first tear could fall. Draping an arm over her shoulders in a comforting gesture, he pulled a handkerchief from his pocket and offered it to her in gallant desperation. "Don't cry, okay?"

"Okay," she said as the first drop rolled down her cheek.

"Oh..." He gently dabbed away the teardrop with the handkerchief. "This really has got you off-kilter, hasn't it?"

She nodded, fighting the tears, fighting the urge to turn her head into his shoulder and sob, fighting a burgeoning longing to kiss him long and hard and empathetically. Who would have thought Kurt McCauley could be so *nice?*

KURT HATED to see anyone cry. He especially hated it when he didn't see it coming, and until a minute ago Emily had seemed fine. Smiling, laughing, aggravating. Then suddenly, she mentioned her great reverence for the institution of marriage, and *wham!*

Tears. "This has to do with your folks," he said, figuring that was the only possible explanation. "You think they're upset."

She nodded again, and he watched her hair brush his sleeve, watched the strands catch on his shirt and splay across his arm, watched as her head dipped close to his shoulder. He lifted a hand to press her face against his chest but stopped, remembering last night's kiss, remembering last night's dreams, remembering lots of things about last night.

"Don't cry," he said, awkwardly patting the air. "Your parents will understand. We'll just tell them the truth. Or you can tell them whatever you want and I'll back you up."

She nodded a third time, sniffed, breathed in, out, shivered...and Kurt wondered what he was doing, standing there, patting the air, hesitant to touch her, afraid to offer the only comfort he knew how to provide. She snuffled softly, wiped at her wet cheeks, cried a little more...and he understood that it was because of him, somehow. With the same strokes he used to gentle an animal, he brushed his hand through her hair over and over and pressed her head tenderly against his chest. She trembled, then the tears stopped and she went still. He let out the breath he'd been holding in a long, relieved sigh. Okay, he thought. One crisis averted.

But when she lifted her head and whispered a shaky thanks, Kurt knew this wasn't over. The tears were still there in her eyes, her lips quivered a little when she made a good effort to smile at him, and she looked suddenly so fragile. But it was the stirring of his own heart that alarmed him, then the unanticipated longing to kiss the tears from her cheeks, to kiss her eyes, her lips...her.

He had no right to complicate her life by kissing her now. He had no excuse, no ulterior motive other than that he wanted to make her feel better. Wait. He wanted *her* to feel better? Who was he kidding? He just plain wanted to kiss her.

So he did.

Her lips parted in the instant before he lowered his head and captured them with his own. The kiss went wild and sweet on him in a split second. Wild with warmth and sweet with passion. Kurt wondered—for the umpteenth time—what in hell he was thinking to kiss her at all, much less like a man starved for a taste of her. His only consolation was that she kissed him back with at least as much hunger and considerably less hesitation.

Which only proved that women were emotional land mines, and he had no business kissing this one, in particular. She was, however temporarily, his wife. But that didn't stop the kiss. Not at all. Her chair swiveled, and instead of the head-to-shoulder angle, he found himself with full frontal contact. Well, not *full* frontal, maybe, but the possibility was definitely there. Especially when her hands slid across his shoulders and her arms went around his neck and with a low groan he pulled her out of the chair and into his embrace.

The red sweater crawled up between them, a wedge of cotton fabric to remind him that beneath it, she had skin that would be warm to the touch and silky soft. She had warm, soft breasts, too. He remembered the curves, the weight of one resting in his palm, and his hand was diving toward the hem of the sweater when the knocking started. At first, he dismissed the tap, tap, tap as the sound of his heart rapping enthusiastically against his ribs, but when Emily detached her hands, her arms and her lips from him, he realized there had been someone outside the office, knocking on the door.

"Emily, I— Oh!" Renetta stopped cold in the doorway.

"Y-yes?" Emily said, self-consciously straightening her sweater and smoothing her hair…and behaving with the self-awareness of a woman who'd just been thoroughly kissed. Even though Kurt didn't feel like that kiss had been nearly thorough enough.

"I'll come back in a…a few minutes."

Renetta made her escape. With a sigh, Emily sank back into the chair while Kurt moved to the edge of the desk, where he couldn't readily reach her and pull her back for a more thorough kiss. "She probably thought I was helping you get something out of your eye," he said. "Either that, or you were trying to read my lips."

Emily treated the possibilities to a discouraging silence.

"She might believe you were teaching me mouth-to-mouth resuscitation."

"I think she knows exactly what we were doing. Which puts her one up on me." Emily sighed. "Well, if our goal was to confuse people today, I'd say we're doing a bang-up job."

Kurt was about as confused as anybody, but he saw no point in admitting it. Especially as he hadn't a single feasible excuse for having just kissed her. He did have enough sense, though, to realize he needed to call off their bet. Much more of this morning, noon and night business and they were going to wind up in bed together for real. Which would compound their original mistake by about a trillion million. He'd end the wager somehow with her thinking it was her idea and not his. Shoot, he'd even let her have the car...but not the endorsement. He just flat didn't want to see men walking around wearing his name on their butts. "Emily," he began. "Maybe it's time we—"

*Ching-ling. Ching-ling.* The front door chime meant customers, and Kurt knew he'd already lost her attention. But that was okay. He could talk his way out of this on the way to her folks' house. Or on the way back, for that matter. It didn't have to happen this minute. As long as he kept his lips off hers, they'd be all right.

"McCauley!" It was Max Thurman's deep bass, sober this time but just as thick. "You in here?"

"Yeah, McCauley!" Steve Cooper seconded the question. "We heard a rumor you turned into a *husband!*"

The men laughed loudly, and Kurt could hear Renetta's timid voice. "May I help you?"

"Excuse me," Kurt said to Emily. "I've got to go sell these guys some hats."

"Be sure they're the expensive ones."

He stopped in the doorway to wink at her. "The best you carry."

"Oh...and Kurt?"

"Yeah?"

"We should mark up what just happened as—as another misjudgment. Let's forget it ever even happened, okay?"

"Nothing happened just now," he assured her. "Nothing at all."

But of all the misleading statements he'd made today, that was the only one he knew for certain was a lie.

# Chapter Eight

"And it just seemed like the right thing to do at the time." Emily wrapped up her why-I-married-Carolina's-old-boyfriend saga and looked to see how her mother was taking it.

Ruth Ann Dawson pulled a pan of hot rolls from the oven and dumped them onto a plate. She set the empty pan in the sink, picked up the plate and perused the browned rolls critically. "All right," she said. "I don't know if this food will be fit to eat, but go ahead and call the men to the table."

"Mom?" Emily asked. "Aren't you going to say something about what I just told you?"

Her mother stopped halfway to the dining room table, the plate of rolls in one hand, a platter of pork chops in the other. "Oh," she said with a smile. "Congratulations."

"Mom!"

The pork chop platter met the tabletop with a heavy thunk, and the rolls were settled next to it.

"Well, Emily, it is sort of funny. You marrying Kurt McCauley when you used to claim he was the best reason God ever gave women for staying single."

If she'd known how often her words were going to come back and kick her in the rear, she'd have gone through life without opening her stupid mouth. "He still is," she stated, opening it again. "And I'm not really *married* to him. I just went through a—a ceremony with him."

"You're married to him if the State of Nevada has to grant you an annulment to get you unmarried. It's like being pregnant. You either are or you're not. And if you went through a ceremony *and* you're living with him—even if it is to win a bet—then like it or not, you're married to him." Ruth headed to the kitchen for the bowls of green beans and potatoes.

Emily followed on her mother's heels. "Cousin Milton said it could take as long as four months to get the annulment. Maybe even longer."

"Have you considered talking to another attorney? One who maybe *passed* the bar exam?"

"Milton passed, Mom. It just took him a few tries." More than a few, actually, but... "Besides, you know Dad says we should keep our business and legal dealings within the family."

"Yes, I know what he says." Ruth brushed past, a huge bowl of vegetables in each hand. "And I'm sure your cousin will manage to get you that annulment sooner or later." She placed the bowls on either side of a silk flower centerpiece. "What do you think, Emily? Here?" She switched the bowls. "Or here?"

As if vegetable placement mattered. "There," Emily said, not paying much attention. "So you're okay with this? You're not mad at me or upset that I married him?"

"Well, of course not. You just got through telling me you got married because it seemed like the right thing to do." Ruth rearranged the vegetables again, putting the bowl of potatoes where the bowl of green beans had been and vice versa. "You're absolutely right. They looked better the other way." She switched them back and surveyed the table with a skeptical eye before she lifted a smile to Emily. "Please stop worrying, dear. Kurtis is a fine young man. Your father and I have always liked him, and we're delighted to have him as our son-in-law."

"It's temporary, Mom. Do *not* get attached to the idea, okay?"

"What idea?" Ruth moved the centerpiece a little to the left. "Oh, I've been meaning to tell you what I heard at the beauty shop the other day. Christa Swift is pregnant again. This will be her fourth. She graduated with you, didn't she?"

As if Ruth couldn't name everyone in Emily's high school class forward and backward. "Yes,"

Emily said, "and she was pregnant then, too. Don't you have any advice for me at all?"

Ruth counted the place settings—one, two, three, four—then she turned and patted Emily's cheek. "Use birth control."

Emily sighed long and forlornly. "This is turning into a Greek tragedy."

"Oh, don't be so dramatic. I think it's all wonderfully romantic...even if you are getting an annulment." Ruth repositioned each chair in turn. "Think of it this way, honey. You undoubtedly saved Kurt from a nasty court date with Farrah Phillips *and* you snatched him right out from under your sister's nose."

Emily raised her chin. "My *sister* is on her *honeymoon,*" she said, then stopped, struck by a sick feeling. "Carolina *is* still on her honeymoon, isn't she?"

"Well, of course, she is, sweetie. You know Carolina. She isn't going to give up ten more days of shopping and sunning herself in the Carribean just to rush home and make you miserable."

"Right," Emily muttered under her breath. "Plenty of time to do that once the honeymoon is over."

"She'll do that once her honeymoon is over," Ruth said, having no clue she was seconding Emily's opinion. "Would you go get the salt and pepper, please? Richard!" Ruth's voice pelted across the hall to the living room. "You and Kurtis come to supper. Oh, and Emily?" The voice dropped to normal volume. "Get the butter out of the fridge, please."

Seasonings in hand, Emily bumped the refrigerator door shut with her hip just as her mother breezed into the kitchen and opened it again. "I wasn't kidding about the birth control," Ruth said as she pulled out a Jell-O salad. "I am not ready to be a grandmother, even though I do think you and Kurtis will make beautiful children when the time comes."

"That time is never coming, Mom. Trust me."

Ruth pulled out a serving spoon and stuck it in the Jell-O. "Never say never, sweetie. Kurtis is a very attractive young man, and you are a healthy young woman, and who would have thought the two of you would ever get together in the first place? It's only natural that you'd want to—well, these things do happen, you know."

Emily lost what little appetite she'd had. It was pretty bad when even her mother believed she couldn't resist sleeping with the man. "Celibacy is very effective." It was all she could think of to say.

"I THINK we squeaked by pretty well." Kurt drove the Mustang—which had been fully admired and commented upon by her father—with the top down and the hot breeze whipping Emily's hair in all directions. "Your dad didn't threaten to break every bone in my body if I looked at you cross-eyed or anything like that."

"He took it for granted you knew," she said, not caring that her hair was in her eyes, still unsettled by the way her parents had accepted Kurt into the family like the prodigal son. Emily hadn't wanted them to run him off the property on a rail, but a less enthusiastic welcome would have been okay. "If I don't win this car, though, you're in deep trouble. He can be really mean when anybody cheats his baby daughter."

"Really? Hmm. He told me I was nuts if I let you get your hands on this classic."

"A ruse," she declared blithely. "Daddy never says what he really means."

"He offered me cash to keep you, too. Wonder what he was up to with that?"

"Probably plotting to have you pay him to take me off your hands. He can be very devious." Emily silently apologized to her salt-of-the-earth, straight-as-an-arrow papa for the exaggeration. Kurt was, of course, making all this up, anyway. "To be safe, you should probably just concede the bet now and save yourself some bucks."

"I'm sure you're right, but I'll take my chances."

She shrugged. "Suit yourself."

"I always do." He pushed up his hat brim with the pad of his thumb and looked at her, his speculative gaze putting her on instant alert. "I've been thinking, though," he said casually, "that you might be ready to renegotiate our little wager."

"And why would I be ready to do that?"

"Well, for one thing, it's going to get mighty inconvenient for you to stick by my side every day, all day. I have to start working with Melba on some new commands for an upcoming commercial. Plus, Hank is scheduled in a movie that's going to require some pretty intensive training."

"Are you going on location somewhere?" Emily didn't know why she couldn't work up a little bigger thrill over that idea. Having him lose by default wouldn't be as much fun as whipping the pants off him, but it would do in a pinch.

"Not for a few more months, but there's a lot of work to do before that happens. In fact, I'm planning to begin Melba's training tomorrow, and I need to put in some hours with Hank, as well. I've neglected him the past couple of days."

"I thought Ray helped you with the training."

"He exercises Hank, works with him when he has time, but Ray has his hands full running the ranch. I have a couple of assistant trainers I normally work with, but they won't be here for another two weeks."

"Hmm," Emily said, unconcerned. "Guess you're going to be putting in some long hours, McCauley. A full day at the store and then home to work some more." She clicked her tongue with mock sympathy. "*You* are going to be one tired cowboy."

He smiled, his mustache lifting at the corners. "Where I go, you go...darlin'. Which is the only reason I mentioned changing the terms of the bet in the first place."

"How considerate of you, Kurtis, but I'll manage. You know what Annie Oakley says. Anything you can do, I can do better."

The mustache pulled tight with a frown. "Look, Emily, we should have ironed out a few of these details before we got involved in this morning, noon and night business. And it's not as if you haven't already chickened out on the night part of it, anyway."

She raised her chin. "Chickened out?"

"You're not sleeping with me, so technically—"

"*Chickened out?*" She told herself to shut up right then, before... "You think I'm too *chicken* to share a bed with you?"

He cut his gaze from the road to her. "That's kind of obvious, wouldn't you say? But that's not what I was getting to. I thought, considering our conflicting schedules, that I'd just be a nice guy and let you have the car before this whole—"

"Whoa, there, Mr. *Nice* Guy. Wait just a doggone minute."

"—living together routine makes us crazy."

"Makes *you* crazy, you mean." Emily didn't know what chicanery he was trying to pull off, but he was not getting out of this without saying a loud and hearty uncle. "What is this, Kurt? Are you saying you quit? That I win the car and the endorsement?"

The mustache drew even tighter as his frown grew. "I'm *willing* to call it a draw and give you the car, but that's all I'm suggesting."

"You'll *give* me the car." She did not know how he kept the hat from blowing off his head, but the fact that it didn't was incredibly annoying. "Well, thank you very much, but I don't want you to *give* me the time of day. I'm going to win this vehicle and the endorsement without any grandiose gestures from you!"

"Grandiose? I'm trying to be a gentleman about this, Emily, and you're not making it easy."

"A crash course in manners wouldn't make it easy for you, Kurt. All I want to know is are you giving up, throwing in the towel, waving the white flag and in particular, crying uncle?"

"No!" he snapped. "The bet holds, damn it. Morning, noon *and* night. The bathroom is the *only* place we do not go *together.*"

"Fine," she said with a careless shrug, wishing she'd kept her mouth shut from the get-go. "I have to be at the store early tomorrow. At seven."

"I have to work Hank first. Be ready at six."

Damn. "That doesn't allow much time to shower and change," she pointed out, regrets already flooding in. "Maybe we should make it five."

He glared at the road ahead. "Want to go for four-thirty?" he asked through clenched teeth.

At that point, Emily belatedly stopped talking.

SHE was going to drive him crazy. Out of the bunkhouse, loony as two moons crazy. If they weren't already getting an annulment, he'd ask for a divorce. Hell, he'd demand it. Kurt offered another strawberry to Hank, who took it from his palm with a soft whuffle. "I was just starting to think of her as human, too," he said, rubbing the horse's velvety nose. "Plus, now I have to *sleep* with her."

Sharing a bed with Emily wasn't going to be conducive to sleeping, however. Kurt knew that, and figured she did, too. She had great legs, nice breasts, a saucy smile and a kiss that was easily hot enough to fry a man's good intentions even before he got into a bed with her. But this was strictly a hands-off agreement. She might be making him nuts, but he wasn't crazy enough to go loving on her. She'd have him roped and hog-tied in nothing flat.

How in heck had he ever gotten mixed up with the woman? Argumentative didn't begin to describe her. And stubborn. Lord, she was stubborn. Nothing like Carolina, who'd always been easy to get along with. "She even outshines you in the mule-headed department," he told Hank, who tossed his head at the word *mule*. "She's probably in the bedroom right now putting a brick wall down the middle of the bed to make sure I don't accidentally touch her."

He'd snuck out of the house while she was in the bath, partly because he needed some space, partly because he didn't want to be in the bed when she got in it. This was all crazy. If she hadn't been so quick to jump to conclusions, she could have been at her own house now with the classic Mustang, probably even the rights to market the McCauley name if she'd played her cards right. And he could have had his place to himself again. No woman taking over his space. No soft voice to distract him. No bare shoulders or long legs to admire. No spicy-sweet scents lingering in the air. No feisty female who wouldn't fall into line when he gave the command to heel.

But Emily didn't want him to *give* her the car. She wanted to *win* it. Kurt had never known a woman more troublesome. Or more aggravating. Or more...challenging. Emily might be a lot of things—most of them irritating—but she didn't allow him to forget she was around, that was for sure. With other women, Carolina for instance, he didn't half-try to be charming. A little effort, a little sweet talk and—*bingo!*—she was nothing but smiles for him.

Not Emily. Why, she'd probably love to see him

so much as lift a finger to charm her. As if he had any inclination to do that. Ha. Sweet-talking her would be like…like dancing with a rattlesnake. Or cozying up to a cactus.

Hank nuzzled his pockets, looking for more berries, and Kurt produced the last one. With an appreciative snort, Hank lipped the strawberry from Kurt's palm and sighed his pleasure. There'd been a time when Kurt hadn't known if he could train this animal. It had taken patience and strategy to bring Hank from an impulsive, skittish colt to the magnificent, responsive stallion he was today. Kurt had spent a lot of time watching Hank, learning his moves, figuring out what made him tick before he'd decided to start training him. And what a payoff. There wasn't another horse like Hank anywhere in the world. Smart, spirited, proud as a judge but gentle as the wind in autumn. A horse worth waiting a lifetime to own.

The idea came to him then. Out of the blue. As crazy as any notion he'd ever had on a starlit night. He'd train Emily. He'd watch her and learn her likes, her dislikes—well, he already had a good handle on the dislikes—and he'd figure out how to charm that car right out from under her if it was the last thing he ever did. No snippy female was going to get the best of him. Not in this lifetime.

"Kurt?" Emily's voice called to him from the back porch. "There's a phone call for you."

He nodded, even though she wasn't there to see his acknowledgment. "See you tomorrow, old son." With a last affectionate pat on Hank's nose, Kurt turned toward the house and a contest he was going to win with patience and strategy. He'd have Emily eating out of his hand before the week was out.

And the week after that, he'd own the Mustang, free and clear. *Uncle, my aunt Aster.*

How DID SHE get herself into these things?

Emily gauged the distance from the doorway to the bed and from her side of the bed to Kurt's. She was an idiot. There was no other explanation for it. After setting him straight about where she would and would not sleep, here she was, maybe ten feet from being in bed with him. And there was no one to blame but herself.

She could have been in her own little house preparing to get into her own little bed. Alone. She could have gone to sleep thinking about her own classic car parked in her own driveway. Alas, no garage. But she could have built one. With her own bare hands, for a lot less trouble than she was currently mired in. Kurt had *offered* her the car—he probably would have given her the endorsement, too, if she'd only played her cards right—and she'd been so incensed at his patronizing words that she'd turned him down. No doubt about it, his idiocy was rubbing off on her.

"Are you going to stand there all night?" He was in bed, watching her, sitting with his back against the headboard, a hint of good humor peeking at her from under that damn mustache, his arms crossed over his bare chest. *Bare.* Hadn't he ever heard of pajamas?

"No," she said in a more defensive tone than she intended. "I was just wondering if I forgot something in the other room, that's all."

"Couldn't be something to sleep in. You look like you're wearing every article of clothing you could find."

"I do not," she informed him. "I'm only wearing—" a pair of men's lounge pants she'd found in a closet, a man's long-sleeve shirt from the same place and the robe she'd brought with her from home, plus house shoes with bunny ears and faces "—my normal nightclothes."

"You're going to get pretty hot if you wear all that to bed."

"I'm cold-natured," she said, giving him her best haughty expression. "I'll be quite comfortable, thank you."

He wasn't fooled…as witnessed by his wide grin. But then, she wasn't here to fool him. She was here to share his bed. It would have served him right if she'd worn something sexy, short and skimpy…or nothing at all. That would have separated the men from the boys in this room. That would have wiped the grin off his face.

On second thought, she'd probably made the best possible nightwear choice available under the circumstances. Inhaling sharply, she walked to the vacant side of the bed. "Scoot over, McCauley," she said as she slid under the covers. "And stay on your own side."

"I'm a restless sleeper," he informed her. "Some nights I'm all over this bed."

"You put your big toe anywhere near me and you'll be pulling it out of your nose."

"Making threats will give you bad dreams."

She rolled her head on the pillow so he'd get the full affect of her frown. "This *is* a bad dream, but I'm going to combat it by thinking of what color stitching I want the words *McCauley Khakis* spelled out in."

"What about chicken-heart yellow?"

Somehow, someway, he was going to pay for this. "I'm leaning toward smart-ass apricot. But I may change my mind and go for My-Mustang red."

He laughed and slid down, playing a bit of tug-of-war with the covers as he got settled. "We're quite a pair, Emily Dawson, and if I'm still alive in the morning, I'll make breakfast."

Like she wanted to eat at four-thirty?

Melba, having sniffed her way into the room, jumped onto the bed, barked excitedly and began digging at the bunched covers around Emily's feet like a crazed treasure seeker. No amount of pushing or scolding could make her quit scratching, so with a sigh Emily tossed off the covers, sat up, and one after the other pulled the bunny slippers off her feet and pitched them to the ecstatic terrier. "There, fussbudget," she said to the dog. "Are you happy now?"

Melba settled at the foot of the bed with her booty, and as Emily wrestled once more with the covers and snuggled down, Kurt reached over and scratched her back. She stiffened, feeling a startling, soft pleasure that had absolutely no business being in this bed with them. "What do you think you're doing?" she asked.

"Well," he replied. "It worked for Melba."

Emily smiled, despite every reason to turn over and sock him with her pillow. "You're a pervert, McCauley."

"Maybe," he agreed. "But you're hot and going to get hotter before the night is over."

Not entirely because of her several layers of clothing, either. But she could hardly admit that to him. "Mind your own business," she said.

So he turned over and went to sleep.

FROM FIVE O'CLOCK the following morning until sundown four days later, Kurt watched Emily. At the store, he played the assigned role of general flunky and paid attention to the way she handled responsibility. At the ranch, he took charge, setting tasks to test her mettle, her patience, the range of her good humor and the incidents that triggered her quick temper as well as her warm laughter. At meals and after dinner, he drew her into conversation and reflection, trying to find the areas of their disagreement, the common ground of experience, the opinions they shared—and didn't.

At night…ah, at night he listened to the flip-flop of her ridiculous bunny slippers—now minus ears and whiskers thanks to Melba—and to the gargle of mouthwash before bed, to her sigh when she finally relaxed beside him and to the deep, even rhythm of her breath when she fell asleep. He learned the soft moue of her expression just before she awakened and the shape of her back as she curled on her side beside him. He loved the moments when she first got into bed and hunkered down on her side like a soldier in the trenches, resolute in her determination to share his nights and win the wager by her own sheer stubbornness. It was in those moments that he felt the swirl of a heady awareness, recognized anew that she was as conscious of his presence in the bed as he was conscious of hers. Sexual attraction was a rowdy bedfellow and took up a lot of space. Kurt knew with an inner certainty that Emily's conflict with it mirrored his. He had not a doubt that she was thinking the same sensual thoughts, pushing away the same inappropriate desires, telling herself she was crazy to feel what she was feeling.

Which was true. Physical attraction had no place in their wager. Would make a bad situation worse. A lot worse. But still it was there. Like the spicy-sweet fragrance that seemed to have moved into every corner of his house, every corner of his mind.

It didn't take half a day to figure out that she wasn't a morning person, and discovering that she liked her coffee polluted with milk, sugar, cinnamon and vanilla was a simple matter of watching while she doctored it up. It took longer to establish that she loved sunlight and freshly starched denim. She always ate breakfast—even if it amounted to nothing more than an orange and a bite of toast. Other meals—no matter how tastefully prepared or delectably presented—she picked at, pushing food around her plate like a slow-motion derby. She enjoyed cooking whenever she could spread the cookbooks, pans, ingredients and utensils around the kitchen, and she hated having to fix anything in a hurry. She drank a tall glass of iced tea or, if the day had been particularly chaotic, a beer in the late afternoon. Only one glass or bottle. He could never tempt her to have a second, no matter how hot the temperature or how bad the day had been. She gave him hell on a regular basis, fussing if he made a lot of noise or startled her by walking in unannounced. She refused to go into the bathroom he used, telling him it was teeming with male *cooties*. She made the bed every morning the minute he got out of it and consistently tallied a bill charging him a dollar every time she did. He never paid, but she kept a running tab on the dresser where he was most likely to see it every time he walked by. Emily had aggravation perfected to an art form and practiced it with unabashed glee. And Kurt discovered he rather enjoyed watching her do it.

At the end of the first week, when they'd been married eight days, he ordered flowers for her, telling her it was to celebrate their being one week closer to getting an annulment, which was moving at Milton's breakneck pace, which in turn meant progress was exceedingly unpredictable. Emily loved the flowers. She didn't tell him so. She didn't have to. The delight at receiving such a surprise sparkled in her eyes, the sheer novelty of it shone in her smile, and Kurt's heart beat faster just to look at her.

Observing Emily became his habit and his pastime, and if they hadn't been married, if this silly bet wasn't always there between them, Kurt thought he might have enjoyed romancing her for real.

Instead of just to win the bet.

# Chapter Nine

Jeannie walked into Emily's office and stopped just short of the door. "Get your purse," she said, nononsense hands on no-nonsense hips. "I'm taking you out to lunch."

Emily looked up, tilting her head to see around the spring bouquet of flowers on her desk. "Can't. Too much work to—"

"We can do this nice or I can get nasty," Jeannie said. "But one way or another, we're going to lunch."

Put like that, Emily got her purse, relieved in a way that someone had finally cornered her. She knew what this was about, knew that her marriage to Kurt was still the number-one gossip in town, knew her friends were astonished that she was living at the ranch with him, understood that Jeannie was the designated interrogator for the group. She also knew she couldn't, under the terms of their wager, go to lunch without Kurt—which would really confuse the issue. Unless Jeannie could bully him into not going with them.

"I'll see if Kurt's ready to go," she said, and didn't even make it to the door before Jeannie closed it in her face.

"We'll talk here." Settling her back against the door, Jeannie crossed her arms and waited for an explanation. "You first."

"You don't want Kurt to join us?" Emily asked in a final stab at feigning innocence.

"I want to know what state of holy matrimony you've entered into, Emily, because this is beginning to seem like a freaky episode of *The Twilight Zone*."

Emily set down her purse and propped an arm on the file cabinet. "Kurt and I have a bet. If I win, I get the car—you've seen the Mustang?"

Jeannie nodded.

"Well, we were the winning couple in the KLAS radio station's contest, and the classic Mustang was the prize." Emily paused. "You've probably heard that, too."

Again, Jeannie nodded. "I remember seeing that poster at the wedding chapel, but I didn't think you entered the contest."

"Me, either, but they took the names from the marriage licenses, so if a couple got married, they were automatically entered. Anyway, we won the car, and now I'm going to win it from Kurt. Plus the McCauley endorsement for the clothing line."

"And if you don't win?"

"Not a possibility."

"Humor me."

"He gets the car."

"And?"

"And free clothes from Dawson's Duds."

Jeannie's expressive eyebrows rose. "Forever?"

Emily shrugged. "Pretty much."

"So what was the bet? That you could make your friends crazy trying to figure out what in Sam Hill you're doing?"

"He bet me that I couldn't get along with him in order to win the car."

Jeannie ran a hand through her short black curls, apparently calculating the odds. "Get along," she repeated slowly. "As in laughing at his jokes or as in not hitting him with a baseball bat?"

"Um..." Emily drummed her fingers against the metal file. "More like the latter."

"What's the duration of this bet?"

"Six more days," Emily said, then added, "morning, noon and night."

Jeannie blinked. "What does that mean?"

"It means just what I said. I have to *be* with him so I can *get along* with him. Otherwise it wouldn't be much of a wager."

"You're not with him now," Jeannie pointed out.

"He's in the store. We don't have to be in each other's pockets every second. Just always nearby."

"So *that's* why no one has seen one of you without the other this whole week. I was starting to believe you'd undergone some sort of alien transformation and the two of you shared a brain."

Just a bed, Emily thought. And breakfast. And everything in between. Well, not quite everything. She'd thought the constant togetherness would have her biting her nails to keep from screaming. She'd believed he would get on her nerves in a big way and that once she won the bet, she'd truly have earned the prize. Strangely, though, she wasn't biting her nails, and he wasn't getting on her nerves—well, not much, anyway.

Four days ago, Kurt had changed tactics. He'd stopped razzing her about her hair, her coffee, what she wore to bed. He'd stopped trying to goad her into a temper tantrum and started watching her, instead. And then today...flowers. Whatever he was up to—and she suspected it was no good—he had her on edge.

"One question." Jeannie gave her the don't-lie-to-me-about-this stare. "You're sure he's not holding you hostage out at that ranch of his? Won't let you use the phone to call your friends and let them know you're all right?"

Emily smiled at the absurd notion that Kurt could stop her from doing anything she wanted. "I volunteered to move in with him because he has animals to take care of and I don't even own a goldfish. And of course I can use the phone. I just...haven't.''

"You volunteered to move in with him." Jeannie sounded incredulous at the idea.

"Because of the bet," Emily said in clarification, "I have to live with him to win the bet."

"In other words—" Jeannie cut straight to the chase "—you're sleeping with him to get a car."

"I am not," Emily said indignantly. "I'm sleeping with him to win the bet. No, I mean I'm *not* sleeping with him...well, yes I am. *Sleeping* with him, that is. But that's all. He stays on his side of the bed, and I stay on mine."

Jeannie's jaw dropped. "You're kidding."

"No," Emily said. "I'm not."

"You mean to stand there and tell me you are getting into the same bed with that gorgeous man and *not* having sex with him?"

"Yes," Emily said. "I am."

"You do realize you're destroying one of my all-time favorite fantasies, I suppose? I mean, if you can't count on a man like Kurt McCauley to seduce the most frostbitten heart in the county, what can a gal depend on?" Jeannie looked completely disillusioned for a second, then her expression brightened. "It's not his fault. It's you who's not taking advantage of this amazing opportunity, isn't it?"

"*Amazing opportunity?*" Emily repeated cynically, although she acknowledged privately that there was something in what Jeannie said. The sleeping arrangements at the ranch weren't *entirely* platonic on her side of the bed. Not that she ever touched him, of course. Or even came close to it. But if thinking about it counted… "Believe me, he's not that amazing."

Jeannie's grin was suddenly as big as Arizona. "And how would you know that unless you'd taken him for a test drive? You're conning the whole lot of us, aren't you, Em? I knew you couldn't be as immune to his charm as you let on all these years."

"I am immune," she said quickly. "I am."

But Jeannie was off and running with her theory. "I always figured there had to be a pretty big fire going underneath all that passionate dislike the two of you dished out. Carolina was cool as a cucumber, but you… This is great. Really. I'm happy for you, Emily. It's high time you fell off the wagon train and admitted you've been in love with Kurt since as far back as any of us can remember."

"Why, that's crazy!" Emily denied it even as her stomach plummeted with the possibility. But it wasn't true. Couldn't be true. Jeannie was just speculating along the lines of her own fantasies. "That is the most ridiculous thing you've ever said to me."

Jeannie stopped smiling, apparently seeing the panic in Emily's expression, hearing the note of dismay in her voice. "Oh, yeah, sure. I guess it is pretty ridiculous to think the two of you... Hey, I get carried away with crazy notions like that all the time. You know me. Always shootin' off my mouth and...well, what in the heck do I know? Just because he's perfect for you and you stepped right up to marry him doesn't mean..." She pushed away from the door, dusting her hands as if that would dismiss the whole idea. "It's a good thing you never listen to me, anyway, because you're right. It was a really stupid idea, and I don't know how I came up with it in the first place."

"I don't, either." Emily tried to sound miffed, tried to put a healthy note of scorn into the words, but like the elephant on the table, the idea was there now, and it wouldn't be ignored. "I certainly hope you're not going to repeat it to anyone else." She made a scoffing noise. "As if anyone would believe such nonsense. Me in *love* with Kurt McCauley. Ha! Like that isn't the joke of the century!" *Shut up, Emily,* she thought. *Let it go.* But she couldn't, somehow. It was as if she had to keep talking to convince herself there was no truth in it. "There probably isn't a person in this whole state who'd believe that I could feel anything for that man except the utmost distaste. And he feels the same about me. Why, this past week has been torture, just plain—"

"I get the picture," Jeannie said.

"—awful," Emily finished with a vehemence she was far from feeling. The week hadn't been torture.

It hadn't even been all that inconvenient. She'd even go so far as to admit there'd been moments when Kurt had been tolerably charming...but that didn't mean she was in *love* with him. "Well, it is a nutty idea, Jeannie."

"You're right. It is," Jeannie agreed with a shrug. "I'm sorry I ever voiced an opinion. But don't go thinking I'm going to tell people you're sharing a bed with him but refusing to have sex with him. That would be too cruel for all those women who're out there thinking of you as their role model. I'll just say I heard it straight from the horse's mouth and that you *are* sleeping with him. That ought to keep the hearts palpitating for another week."

"Oh, perfect," Emily said on a sigh.

"Well, jeez, Em. We have to have something to entertain us. And the idea of you and Kurt McCauley married and sleeping together—" Her smile bloomed like a rose at the anomaly of it. "There must be bookies in Vegas right now who're kicking themselves for not taking odds on that one." Jeannie shook her head in wonder. "I wish I'd done it myself."

"I don't see why you have to make such a big deal of this."

Jeannie's eyebrows rose higher than before. "You're awfully touchy all of a sudden. Shoot, if I was the one sleeping with him, I'd be bragging about it to strangers on the highway...and I wouldn't be admitting it was only sleep, either. After all, you *are* married, Emily.''

''I *am* getting an annulment, too.''

''Well, once that happens, maybe you shouldn't brag about sleeping with him anymore.''

Emily straightened. ''Is that all you came down here to find out?''

''Yes.'' Jeannie eyed the bouquet on the desk before snagging the florist's card in her hot little hand. ''That and who's romancing you with flowers.''

Emily lifted her chin.

'' 'Happy anniversary, darlin','' Jeannie read, her voice sharpening with new speculation. '' 'One week and counting...' ''

''That refers to the time left until the annulment is granted,'' she said, totally on the defensive.

''I didn't say a word, Em.''

''But you were thinking.''

Jeannie tucked the card back where it belonged. ''I was *thinking* I'm starving and that we should go get some lunch.''

''I don't have much of an appetite these days,'' Emily said.

''Then you can sit there and watch me flirt with your husband. In fact, if you're sure it doesn't bother you, I may just have him for lunch.''

Emily picked up her purse and opened the door. ''You can do anything with him you want,'' she said. ''I couldn't care less.''

But the words had a false ring even in her own ears.

EMILY prided herself on being levelheaded. Okay, so she sometimes was a little impulsive, but generally speaking, she wasn't easily rattled. Certainly, she'd never thought Kurt McCauley was bright enough to slip anything past her. But here she was at the Hungry Cracker Grill, Fortune City's main claim to fine dining, on what, for all intents and purposes, appeared to be a date with her husband.

Celebrating, Kurt had called it when he'd suggested they go out for dinner. One week and counting, he'd said when *she* suggested they had nothing to celebrate. His mood was cheerful, his manners perfection—he even came around and opened the car door for her!—and Emily could not figure out what he was trying to do. Unless confusing her was his aim.

Truth be told, she was confused even before the evening began. From the time Jeannie had made the remark, Emily hadn't been able to stop the litany of words going around in her head. *A pretty big fire— passionate dislike—in love with Kurt.* Not that she believed for an instant there was anything to the theory. Opposites didn't necessarily attract. She had enough sense not to sleep with the enemy.

On the other hand, he *was* the enemy, and she *was* sleeping with him and, even if they were both pretending not to notice, there *was* an undercurrent of attraction going on. Purely physical, of course. What else did they have in common? A mutual love of animals—Hank and Melba, in particular? A history—even if it involved Carolina and a whole series of burning bridges? A marriage license—regardless of how temporary? A wager? A grudging admiration for the other person's stubborn determination?

*Yes. Yes. Yes. Yes and yes.* Emily picked at the food on her plate, hardly aware of what she'd ordered, very aware of the man sitting across the table. She couldn't be in love with Kurt. She'd had such a good time hating him...well, maybe hate was too strong a word. Dislike was better. Passionate dislike. Then the litany started all over again.

"Have you always been such a picky eater?"

She looked up to see Kurt watching her scoot a green bean into a mound of mashed potatoes. "No," she said, because she wished he would stop watching her and she wished he wasn't so damned handsome and she wished she could stop thinking about being in love with him. Which she wasn't. In love, that is. She was, unfortunately, thinking about it. "Lately, I've just lost my appetite, that's all."

"Stress affects some people like that," he said, applying fork to steak.

"I'm not stressed," she stressed. "I'm just not hungry."

He pointed the fork at her. "I hope you're not

dieting, Emily, because that isn't healthy. Plus..."
And here his lips curved into a meltingly tender
smile. "You don't need to lose weight. You're perfect just the way you are."

Definitely, this man was up to no good. "I love
dieting," she said to be contrary. "I do it all the
time."

The fork, with attached square of steak, paused
halfway to his mouth. "You're—" He stopped,
smiled again, although with a little less warmth. "I
don't want to argue with you," he said. "Not tonight."

She was going to get to the bottom of this. "Why
not? Tonight's no different than any other night."

"It's our anniversary."

Emily stopped any pretense of interest in food.
"All right, McCauley, what's this about? And don't
give me that dumb *what?* expression, either. You've
been watching me like I was a hothouse rose all
week. Plus you've been extremely considerate...*and*
nice. There's that basket of flowers you sent, and
you bought mine and Jeannie's lunch, charmed her
socks off into the bargain, and tonight—" she leveled the spoon at him as she added the final indict-
ment "—you opened the car door for me!"

His smile was more dazzling than reassuring. "I
know how to behave like a gentleman, Emily. Does
that bother you?"

"No. Yes." She put down the spoon. "This

whole week has been..." *Strange. Exciting. Fun. Challenging.* Wait a minute. *Fun?* "Strange," she admitted to him.

"Enlightening," he countered. "Interesting, stimulating and ripe with discovery."

"Ripe? That's overstating it some, don't you think?"

He put down his fork, reached across the table and took both her hands in his. A fast-burning fire couldn't have created any more heat, and her skin fairly sizzled in response to his unexpected touch. But she didn't pull away. "What if I said I'd learned some unsettling truths this week?" He squeezed her fingers so tightly they all but squeaked. "What if I said this love-hate relationship we've always nurtured is a little more one than the other?"

Oh, boy. She was in trouble here, but she tried to look into his eyes—those bad-boy bedroom blue eyes—without letting on that a stampede of crazed buffalo had nothing on her rampaging heartbeat. "I'd say...you're trying to romance yourself into a car."

If Kurt had done anything other than laugh, Emily would have recognized him for the lying scoundrel he was. But she was already on edge, already vacillating on a dangerous precipice, and when he laughed with a deep and rich amusement, confusion carried the day.

"I can see I have a ways to go to convince you

I'm worth a second look," he said, sounding frighteningly sincere.

"Rest assured, Kurt, I never take my eyes off you for a second."

The laughter fell away into a persuasive smile. He turned her hands palms up within the cradle of his own and began to stroke them with his thumbs. Emily breathed in…out…in, and could not stop the raw swirl of pleasure inside her. She'd always known he was a master of seduction. She'd always believed she was immune. Man, did she hate finding out she was wrong.

"I don't know how I failed to discover you before now," he said in a voice as caressing as the sensual stroking of her palms.

She swallowed hard, strong-armed a tiny core of resistance. "You were busy discovering Carolina," she reminded him.

"I was an idiot."

No argument there. "You're still an idiot." But she said it with a smile, which he seemed to take as encouragement. "Especially if you think this Romeo routine is going to work with me."

"I never realized you were so distrustful of men, Emily."

"I'm not. I just don't trust you." And she didn't. But if he kept stroking her palms this way, it wasn't going to make a whole lot of difference. "You want to win this bet and you've taken the misguided notion that I can be had for a song and dance.''

"I don't believe that at all.'' His thumbs stilled their scintillating circles and he held her breathless with an unwavering gaze. "I'm not sure you can be *had,* as you put it, at all, Emily. But I think you're worth the effort.''

She'd really had no idea he was this good...or that her heart could beat so fast at such a blatant lie. "I think your nose has grown a foot since we sat down at this table,'' she said. "Maybe a foot and a half.''

His laughter felt every bit as good as a blanket on a cold night. "Can't a husband compliment his wife without being accused of lying?''

"I know a setup when I see one.'' She pulled her hands—finally—out of the embrace of his fingers. "I'll admit you talk a good game, McCauley. I'll even give you credit for not saying anything that I can point to as an outright, bold-faced lie. But I know and you know that this is about our bet. So...cut it out.''

He watched her for a moment, his gaze following her hands from the tabletop to her lap as she brought the napkin to her lips, returned it to her lap again. Emily only hoped he didn't see the way her fingers trembled, couldn't tell how much he'd rattled her. Darn Jeannie for putting this absurd love idea into her head, anyway.

"This isn't about the car," he said softly, bringing her gaze to his. "Or the endorsement."

Truth sounded different from a lie, and this sounded like the truth. It couldn't be. She knew that. But her resistance was ebbing fast, and she somehow wanted to believe him. "It is, too."

"No."

She took a deep breath and called his bluff. "Prove it."

For the space of a dozen riotous heartbeats, he only looked at her. Then, without a word, he pushed back his chair, stood up and came around the table, where he took her hands again and pulled her to her feet. "I only know one way to do this," he said.

Then in front of anyone who chanced to be looking—which was everyone in the restaurant—he bent his head and kissed her. A real kiss, passionate, serious, seductive and thorough.

And if it was a lie, Emily never wanted to know the truth.

KURT FELT as if he was always playing catch-up with Emily. He'd spent the entire week observing her, figuring out what made her tick, and still he was the one who ended up zapped by surprise. Zapped by a kiss was more like it. What had ever given him the idea that he could get around her with a dab of charm, a smokescreen of sweet talk? She hadn't been fooled for a second. Oh, she gave a good impression of it, sure. But from the first compliment out of his mouth, she'd known where he was headed, and she'd beaten him getting there, too, taking him in completely on her way.

So how come he was pacing the bedroom and feeling danged guilty for setting out to fool her in the first place? Hell. For a few minutes there at the restaurant, he would have sworn he *was* in love with her. She'd led him straight down the bridle path without so much as a blink, displaying all the soft glances and shy, startled smiles of a woman in love. She'd even trembled like a leaf during the kiss he'd so deliberately set out to give her. Or maybe it had been he who was trembling.

Another dynamite kiss, even before he'd felt the sweet, slow dance of her tongue against his. In public, too. Clearly, Kurt decided, he was outclassed and outmaneuvered in this contest. And if she'd take the win and go home, he'd start yelling uncle so loud she'd be able to hear him all the way into the bathroom, where she was changing into her nightly armor.

It was too late for a graceful exit from the game, though. He couldn't even return to their adversarial positions without looking like a complete jerk. And a liar. Oh, who was he kidding? He *was* a jerk and a liar and a complete idiot to have gotten into this mess in the first place. That annulment couldn't come through fast enough to suit him.

Then she opened the bathroom door and walked down the hall toward him, and his brain cells abandoned his head to take residence much lower.

Man, oh, man, was he ever in trouble now.

*Chapter Ten*

It was one thing to kiss a man in the Hungry Cracker Grill. It was another thing altogether to approach his bed adorned in terry cloth and a few sketchy plans for seduction. The way Emily figured it, if Kurt had intended to romance her all the way into a genuine love scene, he'd have followed that kiss up with more hand holding, sweetly told lies and enough kisses to send her good sense boot-scootin' down the highway. But he hadn't. He *had* opened the car door for her and made a point of pointing it out, but other than that he'd practically ignored her on the trip home.

Emily didn't know what he'd been up to, kissing her like that in front of God and everybody. He'd probably expected her to get so mad she'd lose her temper—and the bet. But she didn't care one way or the other what he'd meant for that kiss to convey. She *did* care that she'd responded to it. Responded *passionately* to it. Been left reeling by it. His kiss had changed everything for her, left her with questions she couldn't answer, set her to analyzing feelings she hadn't even known she felt, scuttled possibilities and denials around her brain like a pinball.

All she deduced was more questions and a plan to kiss him again...in private and while she had her wits about her. It wasn't that she really wanted to test Jeannie's theory. After all, finding out she was in love with Kurt McCauley would not exactly make her day. Still, she had to do something. She couldn't spend the whole night in bed beside him wondering if she were so desperate for Prince Charming that a kiss from a frog could seem like the real thing.

Her plan was simple. Mainly because she was too nervous for anything complicated. She would throw him off guard, make him nervous if she could. She planned to rattle his cage with a little cleavage, a glimpse of thigh and see how he liked being romanced.

Of course, he was a man, and that pretty much answered that question. But even if he ran screaming down the hall at the thought of being seduced by her, she figured he would at least participate long enough for her to discover what she needed to know.

He'd stopped pacing the bedroom floor the minute she walked into the room and stood staring at her with a stun-gunned look in his eyes. So far, so good, she thought. The last time she'd walked past him wearing a towel, he hadn't even noticed.

"Hi," she said, as if she were barely aware of his presence.

"Hi," he answered on a sharp exhale. "You forgot to put on your pj's."

"No, I didn't." Lifting one bare shoulder in a shrug, she began to turn back the covers. "I'm feeling sort of—*hot*—tonight."

If it hadn't been for a cricket's persistent chirp, she probably could have heard him gulp.

"You're going to sleep in a towel?"

"Of course not." She gave him an offhand smile. "Once the lights are out, I'm going to take it off."

Even the cricket stopped chirping for a moment. "Emily?" Kurt said, his tone making it a full-blown question.

She reached back with both hands to pull the weight of hair off her neck, aware that the movement gave maximum lift for minimal cleavage, and decided it was a good thing seduction was not her bread and butter, because he didn't appear to be bamboozled by her display of charms. "Yes, Kurt?"

"Are you wearing something under that towel?"

She let her shoulders lift with studied indifference. "What would be the point?"

His chin came up. "Okay, what's this about?"

"Going to bed," she suggested amiably.

"This is payback for the restaurant, isn't it?"

She raised an eyebrow. "Oh, the food wasn't *that* bad."

"Or *that* good. This is about me kissing you in front of all those people. I know it is."

She gave him the benefit of the doubt. "I suppose you could be right. I really haven't thought about it."

"Oh, yes, you have. You would not get into this bed with me unless you meant for something to happen, Emily."

"I've done it every night this week."

"Fortified by forty pounds of clothes," he said, clearly struggling with her modus operandi. "I definitely would have noticed if you'd come to bed naked."

Okay, so he wasn't turned on by long sleeves and lounge pants. Like she hadn't known *that*. "I was naked on our wedding night," she said, which, technically, wasn't a lie.

"And I noticed," he said, which *was* a lie even if he didn't know it. "You told me so."

"Yes, but you forgot later, so it doesn't count."

He assessed the situation, his gaze dipping to her thighs, rising to the knot that secured the towel, dropping again to her legs. "If I thought for one second that you...." He laughed. It was a little on the strangled side, but it was a laugh. "You've taken some low roads this week, Emily, but this one is really beneath you...no pun intended."

"Oh, and I suppose you were on the *high* road back there in the restaurant? Gazing into my eyes, holding my hands, kissing me like you meant it? Come on, Mr. Romance, at least be honest.''

He got that stubborn look he wore so well. ''What if I said I *was* being honest? That I *meant* everything I said.''

Just the thought that there was one one-hundredth of a percent chance he was telling the truth sent hope spilling into her heart. Bad sign, she thought. Very bad sign. ''Well, what if *I* said I *am* hot and I only wanted to sleep in something a little cooler?''

''I'll loan you a T-shirt. Hell, you could wear your underwear and look less seductive than you do in that towel.''

*Seductive?* Maybe this wasn't a lost cause yet. ''What do you care what I wear to sleep in, Kurt? Regardless of what I'm wearing—or not wearing— this is the same body you've been sleeping next to all week, and you didn't seem to have any trouble resisting it before.''

''I'm not saying I can't resist it now,'' he said. Then his voice dropped to a husky low. ''I'm only saying I don't want to.''

Emily raised her chin in hopes it would keep her heart from falling at his feet. ''What would you say if I told you I didn't want you to, either?''

''Hot damn?'' he suggested, superbly breaking the spell.

*Men*, Emily thought. ''Men,'' she said, and let her hair drop to her shoulders so her hands were free to double-check the security knot of the towel. "Is sex *all* you ever think about?"

His hand swept through his hair, mussing the hat line, making him look vulnerable and confused and—*oh, hell*—desirable. "No," he said irritably. "Sometimes we think about how women can talk so much and not say a damned thing we can understand."

"Which seems fair, since women have to wonder how a man can suck the romance right out of a very promising situation and then have the gall to turn right around and blame her for it!"

"Wait a minute. You thought this was a promising situation?" He looked doubtful, hopeful and suspicious all in one long gaze. "Look, I know this is probably a really stupid question but...are you by any chance *trying* to seduce me?"

Emily wondered why everything with Kurt had to be so complicated. "Well, it seemed like a good idea when I first walked in here."

He regarded her for a moment while the cricket chirped once, then again. "And now?"

She sighed, wondering why *she* made everything so complicated. "Now I wish I'd walked in and jumped you. Then we wouldn't have had to have this nutty conversation."

His laughter was still slightly strangled, still a bit nervous, but it was also tender and strangely sweet. "If I live to be a thousand, Emily Dawson, I will never, ever be able to predict anything you say or do.''

She knew then. Like the way she knew the difference between a cubic zirconia and a diamond. There were flaws in her feelings for this man, but that's what made the love real. She, Emily Georgia Dawson, was in love with the last man on earth she wanted. The only man on earth she couldn't be in the same room with without wanting to strike up a kickboxing match. The man who was in love with her sister.

Her sigh came all the way from the depths of her heart. ''Let's just forget I—'' But when she looked up he had already crossed from his side of the bed to her side, covered the distance in a few long strides. She clutched the towel over her bare breasts. ''Kurt?''

''I only know one way to do this, Emily,'' he said, and pulled her into his arms. His lips were on hers almost in the same instant, and his kiss was so hard, so deep, so *meant to be* that her knees gave way. He caught her and pressed her closer to his body. His *hot* body. Or maybe it was her body heat that had her skin tingling like a bad sunburn. Except this wasn't bad. This was good. This was *very* good.

He kissed her over and over with frantic, fumbling, *passionate* kisses that flashed and burst like fireworks into her consciousness and rocketed a lusty, lustful ache through her already shaky legs.

His hands seemed to be all over her at once, large, bare and arousing, but it was her hand that grasped his and pressed it to her breast. He was quick, and the towel pooled around her toes almost before she knew it was falling, but that only meant his shirt was in the way. The zipper of his jeans pressed into the flat surface of her belly, his arousal straining hard against her as her fingers worked his shirt buttons, ripping at them, pulling at the material until it tore and at last her palms connected with his chest. His broad, muscled, hair-roughened chest. He was perfect. The right size. Right shape. Right everything.

Okay, so he was the wrong man. She was entitled to make a few mistakes. Well, one, anyway. One night with the man her friends only fantasized about. One purely selfish act of unmitigated lust. So there was a little more than lust on her side. She was going to have to hate being in love with McCauley for the rest of her life. She might as well enjoy it this once. Besides, this had been her idea, even if she hadn't thought it through to its logical conclusion. Or maybe she had but just hadn't admitted it. Either way, her body wanted his so much the longing was like a physical pain inside her, and she meant to have him.

Which was lucky, considering his hands were stroking her in places that really counted and his tongue was doing deliciously sensual things to hers, and if he stopped, she would have to make him start all over again. And again. She tunneled a hand through his hair, loving the weight of it, the texture, intending to hold his lips hostage for as long as she lived, but he broke their kiss to put his lips to her breast, to nuzzle and nip and generally make her insane with desire—which was a pretty good idea, too. Now, if only she could get him out of those jeans.

She had no more than unsnapped the waist when he drew back, hopping on one foot as he pulled off his boots and tossed them carelessly across the room, scaring Melba, who made a startled dash from the room. Dumb dog. Her one chance to see some action in this bedroom and she let a falling cowboy boot distract her. Not that Emily paid more than cursory attention. She was busy offering awkward but eager help to Kurt's efforts in shimmying out of his jeans and underwear. She got caught up in admiring the full extent of the part he usually kept under wraps and shivered when he pulled her roughly into his naked embrace for more long, wet and very erotic kisses.

When eventually he tipped her onto the bed, she was drunk with his kiss, drunk with love for him, drunk out of her mind with wanting him, and when he followed her down, she pulled him hungrily on top of her and wrapped her legs around his. He levered up to look at her, and she knew it was possible to drown in a pair of blue eyes. "We can still stop this," he said, although his voice was husky and thick. "But please God, tell me now."

"I have been trying for six months to get you out of those jeans," she whispered.

"And into a pair of your khakis," he reminded her, sounding nearly as breathless as she.

"Right now all I can think of is getting you into me."

"You have really good ideas," he said. "But I have to get something from the bathroom first." He smiled, and she changed her mind about his mustache. It was perfect, just like the rest of him. "Promise you won't change your mind before I get back."

She frowned, torn between letting go of him and behaving like a responsible adult. Responsibility won, but just barely. Pulling his head down for another full-impact aerobic kiss, she let him break away with a sigh. "You've got fifteen seconds or I start without you."

He kissed her again just to remind her that he'd be worth the wait, then he was gone. Emily counted to ten—twice—before he was back and kissing each toe, then shins, calves, knees, thighs and...*oh, glory,* he knew how to make every second count.

She was certain she was losing her mind when he pushed hard into her and she took him in, cradling him inside her body, loving him with all the pent-up passion of a lifetime and all the regrets yet to come. She was hot. So hot, she could easily believe she'd never be cold again. He was rough and tender and just awkward enough that she knew he wanted to please her, needed desperately to give her pleasure, to love her wildly, passionately and oh, so thoroughly.

Which he did.

Again and again and…again.

"A WEEK AGO, I wouldn't have bet a plug nickel that you and I'd be so good at that." Kurt lounged on his side, head propped on his hand while his other hand—and his gaze—mapped her body for future reference.

"You bet on really stupid things," she said, her voice whisper-soft and throaty with satisfaction.

"I just said I wouldn't have bet." He drew a fingertip across the slope of her breast, around the puckered nipple, down the other side. "That's smart, I'd say, considering…."

"Mm." She moved lazily beneath his touch, let her eyelids droop, her eyelashes graze her cheek.

Kurt didn't want her to sleep. He wanted her awake for all the things he wanted to do to her. He wanted to get lost again in the earthy brown of her eyes, to lose his mind in loving her, to discover a thousand ways to make her sigh with pleasure. It was strange, impossible, incredible to believe how much he had wanted her, how much he still wanted her. Even sated and suffused in physical satisfaction, he wanted her again. His body tensed at just the thought of it. Better, probably, if he thought about something else. "So," he said. "Does this mean we like each other now?"

"Oh, let's not get carried away with this," Emily said. "I mean, it was nice and all, but..."

"Nice? Oh, come on, Emily, we beat *nice* all to pieces. It was great sex. Extraordinary sex. Guinness Book of World Records sex. You just don't want to admit how much you enjoyed it."

"Screaming *yes, yes, yes* doesn't qualify as enjoyment, I guess."

He traced a fingertip circle around her navel, drifted to her waist, dipped lower. "You didn't scream once. You made this cute little *uh-uh-uh* sound, and you did shout *ride me, cowboy!* that one time, but there was no screaming."

Her eyes opened wide at that, and her not-so-sleepy gaze nailed him with new longing. "You're such a liar, McCauley."

"I like to think of it as predicting the future." He leaned closer, wanting merely to keep touching her, watching her as long as she'd let him. "Because I could make you shout impassioned pleas if I wanted to."

"Help, maybe."

He grinned. "You underestimate me, darlin'."

"Hm. It's possible, I suppose, that I might have missed something the first ten times through. You probably ought to go over each step with me a few more times."

"You're toying with me again."

"Not yet, but after about a ten-minute nap, I may reconsider."

"Forget the nap. I'm your husband, and I say it's time for another conjugal visit."

"Get a life."

"I'm sort of partial to the one I have at the moment." He felt her muscles tense under his stroking fingers and smiled. "So, Emily," he said conversationally even though conversation wasn't really what he had in mind. "What does this do to our bet?"

"It means I won."

"Oh, no," he disagreed. "You did not hear me say uncle. Holy Mahoney, maybe. But uncle... definitely, not."

"Think again, cowboy. The bet was that I couldn't get along with you for two weeks, and I believe you just experienced the ultimate in *getting along*."

"No. Nope. Uh-uh. You're still short several days, plus a whole bunch of mornings, noons and nights. It's going to take a lot more *getting along* than you've done so far, too."

"I never knew you were so greedy," she said.

"Of course, I never knew you *talked* so much. All these years, I thought you were a man of action, Kurt. A man of accomplishment. A man who believed in doing, not—"

Put like that, he had to kiss her.

EMILY was still awake when morning broke. Her stomach churned with the stress of a sleepless night and the knowledge that she had fallen in love with the wrong man. So far she hadn't been able to decide when she'd done this unacceptable thing. Maybe ten years ago, when he was still pulling her ponytail. Maybe as recently as last night. As if the when mattered. What did matter was that it had happened. Without her knowledge, permission or intention, her heart had just gone and done it. Fallen flat on its face in love with the last cowboy on earth she had any chance of living happily ever after with.

Turning her head on the pillow, she watched him sleep, hair tumbled onto his forehead, mustache tucked neatly between nose and mouth, his breathing deep and slow and soothing. It certainly wasn't his fault she hadn't been able to sleep. He'd done his best to exhaust her, even waking up once to try again. But she'd only feigned sleep in that lovely tender interlude after lovemaking, allowed him to drift off without her into dreams of whatever it was he dreamed of. Carolina, probably.

Emily felt sick at the thought. But there was no

getting past it. Kurt had gotten drunk because Carolina broke his heart. He'd raffled himself off in the mistaken idea it would prove he didn't care. He'd been ready and willing to marry Farrah in direct response to Carolina's marriage. And he had married Emily, only because at the time he thought she was Carolina. There was no escaping the truth. Kurt still loved her sister, probably was never going to get over her, and Emily had two choices. Play the role of bride by default or cut her losses right now and save what little face she could.

Pride told her she was worth two of her sister and Kurt was damned lucky she had been the one he wound up married to. Pride assured her she should stay, teach this cowboy a lesson in love he wouldn't soon forget, show him how close he'd come to missing out on true romance. Pride made her want to convince him he'd never really loved Carolina at all. Pride practically demanded she prove to him that falling in love with her was everything he'd ever wanted in the first place.

But she loved him, and her heart told her he deserved better than to have to settle for second best. The truth was, so did she.

Emily leaned over, pressed her lips to his forehead, pulled back to drink in the sight of his face one more time. Then she resolutely got out of bed, went into the bathroom and threw up.

*Chapter Eleven*

"My God, Emily, you look awful." Carolina swept into Emily's little house like a Caribbean breeze, looking extraordinarily beautiful in Caribbean corn-row braids and an exotic—and obviously expensive—Caribbean sarong. With matching sandals. Her nails—finger and toe—were painted coral pink and adorned with tiny images of palm trees and sea-shells. She was tanned and glowing from shopping and sunning and doing exactly as she pleased. Honeymooning clearly agreed with her. "I came home early just to check on you," she said, dropping into a chair with the careless grace only a really beautiful woman could get away with. "At some inconvenience, I might add."

"You shouldn't have," Emily said and meant it. "Where's Jon?"

Annoyance settled into a pretty pout on Carolina's face. "Why is that the first thing everyone asks? As if I'm his social secretary or something."

"Well, you are married to him." Emily cast a futile, foolishly hopeful glance at the empty street in front of her house before she closed the door. It had been well over twenty-four hours since she'd slipped out of the ranch house while Kurt slept. She had to accept the obvious—he wasn't coming after her. "And generally, newlyweds like to be together as much as possible. It seems like a fair question to me."

"Well, if you must know, I don't know where he is." Carolina's voice was snappish, cool. "Probably playing golf on that island where I left him."

"You left Jon in Jamaica?"

The pout deepened. "I told you, Emily, I was worried about you."

Which in Carolina's mind probably made sense, but Emily still needed clarification. "You left your husband of barely three weeks in the Caribbean to come home *one* day early because you were worried about *me?*"

"Well, I didn't *know* he wouldn't come with me until I started packing. Then he told me I couldn't go and I said he'd better not try to stop me or he'd be sorry, and then he suddenly announced he was going to stay an extra week, with or without me." Carolina flounced a little in the chair. "He was not very understanding of what you're going through, Emily."

Emily was surprised. Jon must be smarter than he looked. "What am I going through, Caro?"

"You married him," Carolina said as if the answer should have been obvious, taking for granted there was only one *him* they could possibly want to discuss. "After I told you he was only toying with you to spite me, too."

"Before," Emily corrected, wishing she didn't have to talk about this now. Not while she was still heartsick from leaving him. "Actually, we were already married when you left that message on the recorder."

"Well, you'll want to get an annulment," Carolina said, going from point A to point B on her own direct route. "You don't want to be a divorcee. Not at your age. Ruins your chances with the better class of men. Have you talked to Cousin Milton?"

"He's looking into it."

Carolina nodded. "I'll call him this week, see if he can move things along for you." Her lips curved in a smile that had melted men's hearts from Tucson to Turkey. "I think he always had something of a crush on me. I'm sure if I ask him, he'll do his best to get your annulment pushed through."

"I'm beginning to think a quickie divorce would be easier." Emily didn't even want to discuss this with Carolina, who would work out all the arrangements to her personal satisfaction no matter what anyone else had to say about it. But she felt lousy, heart and soul, and she didn't see why Carolina should feel better. "The situation is sort of... complicated."

"Complicated?" Carolina gave a short bark of laughter. "I should say so. What *ever* possessed you to go through a marriage ceremony, Emily? The last time I knew anything about it, you couldn't bear the sight of Kurt McCauley, and suddenly you up and marry him. And him drunk as a skunk, from what I hear, too. Well, it's no wonder I thought it was a joke at first." She eyed Emily with what for Carolina passed as concern. "I'd have come home sooner if I'd had any idea...but I'm here now and I'll do what I can to help."

Emily sighed. It wasn't that Carolina didn't mean well. It was just that she saw only one perspective on life, love and happiness. Her perspective. "I can handle this," Emily assured her sister. "You should just concentrate on your own problems."

"Jon, you mean?" Carolina waved her hand in airy dismissal. "Oh, he'll come after me."

She was so blithely certain of it that Emily felt a familiar pang of envy. Carolina was beautiful, and men had been coming after her since kindergarten. She was a masterful and imaginative manipulator, knowing just the right mix of feminine pique and coy interest. Scarlett O'Hara had nothing on Carolina. Even their father was butter in her hands. Always had been. It was a fact Emily had lived with all her life. She'd watched Carolina charm every male she wanted—and a few she didn't—into falling in love with her. Their devotion was like elixir, and she thrived on the knowledge that once in love, no man would ever quite get over her. Emily had never mastered the technique during the short phase of adolescence when she'd wanted to be just like her older sister. Today was the first time she'd ever regretted it. Kurt would have come after Carolina. Or he'd never have let her leave in the first place. But then, he was in love with Carolina.

"Well, Kurt won't be coming after me," she said. "You can bet the ranch on that."

"After what he's put you through this week? I certainly hope not. He ought to be horsewhipped, humiliating you in front of the whole town. And just to get back at me, too. I am furious about it, and don't think I won't tell him to his face the first time I see him, either." She tossed her beaded braids. "Come after you, ha! Over my dead body."

Emily hadn't felt humiliated in the least. Until now. "That noble sacrifice won't be required, Caro. He has no reason to come looking for me."

"Of course he doesn't. You shouldn't even give it a thought."

"I haven't," Emily lied. "Not much, anyway."

Carolina frowned, considered, asked curiously, "You almost sound like you wish he would."

"Don't be silly. Why would I wish anything so...impossible? Impossibly stupid, I mean."

Carolina might be self-absorbed, but she wasn't completely insensitive. "You're not— You don't still have a crush on him, do you, Em?"

*Still?* Up until a week ago—not counting the six-week lapse in judgment when she was sixteen and basically unaccountable—she thought she'd never had anything except the utmost distaste for Kurt McCauley. Now, suddenly, it seemed everyone except her—and possibly Kurt—had known the true state of affairs. Sheesh, if Carolina had noticed, it must have been glaringly obvious to everyone. Emily pushed away from the door. "No, I don't *still* have a crush on him," she said irritably, sinking into a chair. "I'm in love with him."

"With Kurt?" Carolina giggled, but stopped when Emily didn't join in. "You're kidding."

A shrug was the only answer Emily could make at first, then she managed a short, humorless laugh. "Isn't *that* the stupidest thing you've ever heard?"

Carolina sat straight, leaned forward, segueing seamlessly into her best big sister being sympathetic mood. "No. The stupidest thing I've ever heard is me sitting here rambling on about Kurt when I should have seen right away how miserable you look." She paused. "Well, I did notice that you look awful, but I thought you had a cold or something. I never thought you... You and Kurt. Unbelievable."

"Thanks."

"I didn't mean it like that."

"Yes, you did. Everyone thinks the same thing. It is unbelievable. Even I think so."

"Oh, Emily, these things happen. I didn't mean to fall in love with Jon. Really fall in love, that is. He's such a tyrant, so stubborn about getting his way. For instance, I wanted to go to Cancun on our honeymoon, but he made the arrangements without even asking me. And I wanted to wait and get married at Christmas, but he *insisted* he couldn't wait that long." Her voice softened. "But he's so romantic. He sent me fresh flowers every single day at our little bungalow." She sighed sweetly, smiled to herself, returned to frowning. "Kurt will not send you flowers, Emily. You'll have to live with that. I tried everything short of coming right out and telling him that girls like to receive roses once in a while, but did he take the hint? Oh, no. He's such a—a *cowboy*. But if he's the one you want."

She left it open-ended, as if Emily had an option.

"He sent flowers," she said without thinking.

"Who?"

"Kurt sent me flowers."

"He didn't."

"He did. Last Friday, for our one-week anniversary." She didn't mention the real reason. Carolina didn't need to know everything.

"He sent you flowers for your anniversary," Carolina repeated as if there might be a test. "*Fresh flowers?*"

Emily nodded, then discarded the idea that flowers meant something. If they had, he'd have followed her home. Or at least called to see if she made it safely. Or to ask for his car back. The Mustang had been the only vehicle at her disposal. She couldn't very well have saddled Hank and ridden him home. So she'd driven to her house in the classic car that she'd now lost, fair and square. Leaving a cryptic note that said uncle pretty much canceled any argument, and the fact that it was still in her possession was just a matter of logistics. Kurt would send Ray or one of the other ranch hands to get it sooner or later. She had never really thought he would waste his time fetching it home.

"I can't believe he sent you flowers," Carolina said, obviously stymied by Emily's success in that department. "He must have realized he's in love with you, too."

Life was so simple for Carolina. Emily shook her head. "He's in love with you."

"Well, probably to some degree, but to be honest, Sissy, I never thought Kurt cared all that much about me, and I never really believed we'd ever get married."

It was as much the childhood nickname as the admission that made Emily's heart go soft with affection. They didn't have much in common, and

Carolina could be frustrating, but they *were* sisters, and there *was* a bond. "That's sweet of you to say, Caro, but I don't have any illusions about Kurt being in love with me. Until yesterday, I didn't have any illusions that I was in love with him, either."

"What happened yesterday?"

"He kissed me at the Hungry Cracker."

"In public?" Carolina's eyebrows rose. "Kurt? Well, that ties it. He never kissed *me* in public." She pushed to her feet, a graceful swirl of sarong settling over her hips. "I'm calling him right now."

Emily, unbelievably, laughed. "You're married, Carolina. Kurt isn't going to kiss you now to make up for past omissions."

"I don't want him to kiss *me,* goose. I'm calling to tell him to get his butt over here and kiss you. In private, where it matters."

Emily sobered immediately. "Don't you dare go near that phone." The very thought of Carolina telling Kurt...

"Then you call him. Tell him you expect him at your door with his lips puckered in five minutes or less. You've always been too mealymouthed with men, Emily. You have to set the rules and dare him to break them. Believe me, men love a challenge."

"I am not calling him," Emily said, her stomach roiling at the idea of hearing his voice, of hearing him laugh at her idiocy in thinking he cared how many rules she set. "He isn't in love with me, and that's final."

"Oh, phooey. Men don't know they're in love until you tell them they are," Carolina insisted. "Good grief, Emily, haven't I taught you anything?"

"I'm not like you, Carolina. Men don't act the same way with me."

"That's because you don't expect them to. Now pick up that phone and call your husband. Tell him I made you call, if it makes you feel better."

"Not talking about this would make me feel better. I'm not calling him, and that's final."

"You're *married* to him, Emily. You have to talk to him sometime. Besides, that's the best bargaining chip you've got at the moment."

"I don't want to *bargain* with Kurt. He isn't in love with me, and I'm not going to waste my time trying to convince him he is just because you say so."

"Oh, Emily, do you have to make everything so complicated? He's man. You're woman. For Pete's sake, if you want him, go get him."

Emily wanted him, but she couldn't go get him at that moment if she'd even thought there was a prayer he'd agree to be gotten. Her body routinely tossed up stress the way other people tossed up bad food, and this morning was no exception. She pushed out of the chair and hurried to the bathroom, where she threw up the saltine crackers she'd had for breakfast.

Carolina, who limited her exposure to illness and other yucky things, was waiting in the living room when Emily returned, paler but feeling somewhat better. "You're pregnant," she said.

Emily blinked. "What?"

"You're pregnant," Carolina repeated. "Look at you, pale as a whitewashed fence, throwing up for no reason." She nodded, convinced by her theory. "You're pregnant."

"I'm *not* pregnant." Emily rubbed lotion onto her hands and cheeks. "I throw up when I'm upset." She frowned at her sister. "You know I've always had a nervous stomach."

"I know nothing of the sort," Carolina stated emphatically. "You're not fooling me for one second, Emily. You're pregnant. It's so obvious."

"It is?" Emily looked down, wondering how anyone could tell.

"Well, yes. Of course, it is. You might as well put a message in the *Fortune City News*."

Emily felt her stomach protest this theory with another nauseating roll. "This is not helping my stomach."

"Do you want me to get you some crackers?" Carolina asked with renewed concern. "I've heard that eating saltines before you get out of bed really helps morning sickness."

Crackers. Ugh. "I'm not in bed, and this isn't morning sickness."

"Well, it is morning, and you are sick. What would you call it?"

"Your delusion?"

But Carolina's brain was busy developing a corollary. "Wow, you must have gotten pregnant on your wedding night. Bad luck that you're getting sick so early, but they say it's hereditary, and Mom was really sick when she was pregnant with you, so I guess it's true."

"It's true that you're completely nuts. I am not, repeat *not*, pregnant. It is not, repeat *not*, possible."

"It always happens to women like you who think it couldn't possibly happen to them. You're pregnant, and Kurt's the father."

"I'm not, and he isn't." The sisterly affection vanished like a long shot. "I haven't even slept with a man for years." Emily wasn't about to add any untils to that admission, either. "I'm telling you I just have a nervous stomach."

"You're pregnant," Carolina said again. "Which means Kurt will definitely stay married to you. For the baby's sake. He's very traditional that way."

*Great,* Emily thought. "Luckily he won't have to make that agonizing choice because I am not— cannot be—pregnant with his or anyone else's baby."

Carolina smiled with the superior knowledge of

being older and presumably wiser. "You shouldn't lie to your sister about sex. Everyone in town knows you spent the entire week with Kurt and that you admitted to Jeannie you were sleeping with him. For the record, I never slept with him, but I don't see how you, at your age, could resist him."

"I could, too, resist him. I *did* resist him." Well, mostly she had.

"Oh, sure. Like you really expect me to believe that?"

"You expect me to believe *you* did," Emily said, sure that Carolina and Kurt had had sex many times during their tempestuous romance. "Resist him, I mean. Talk about lying to your sister!"

Carolina gave her braids a haughty toss. "I never had sex with Kurt McCauley, and I don't care if you believe me or not. I just thought that since you're married to him now, you deserved to know. But I swear, Emily, if you ever breathe a word of that to Jon, I'll…I'll disown you."

Emily frowned. "You want Jon to think you had sex with another man?"

"Yes," Carolina said as if it should have been obvious. "It keeps him on his toes, thinking I was promiscuous before he came along. I don't ever want him to be too sure of me."

There was so much faulty reasoning in there, it made Emily's head spin, but trying to explain was beyond her current capability. As if Carolina would ever be persuaded she was wrong, anyway. "That's crazy," was all she said.

"No, what's crazy is you sitting here pregnant and miserable and not being grown-up enough to tell the man who got you that way."

"I am not pregnant," Emily repeated, voice rising.

"I don't believe you."

"Well, I don't believe that you and Kurt never had—" The thought caused another sickly roll in her stomach. "Well, you know."

"We didn't. But you obviously did. And he needs to know he fathered a child."

Emily knew the more she argued, the more convinced her sister would become. So she stopped. "Can we please stop talking about this? I really don't feel very well."

"Mother was sick from the second she got pregnant with you. Really pukey sick. When you were finally born, I didn't see how she could even like you, since you made her sick that whole time."

Emily had heard this story before. "You were too little to remember any of that. You just want me to think she liked you best."

Carolina smiled. "She did."

"You used to get spankings for saying that. Plus Mom would give me a Popsicle every time you said it because she thought it hurt my feelings. But I always knew she liked *me* best."

"Well, she'll like you best now that you're having her first grandchild. It's really unfair, Emily, that you go and get pregnant before I can." Carolina rolled her lovely hazel eyes. "Jon wants to wait until we've bought a house and a new BMW. He's such a yuppie." She glanced at her watch. "I'm going," she said so casually that Emily's self-protective instincts jerked to attention. "I'll tell Mom you're sick—and no, I won't tell her you're pregnant. But not because I think it needs to be some big secret. I just don't want to have to hear the two of you swapping morning sickness stories."

"Carolina," Emily warned, knowing the way her sister worked. "Don't you dare call Kurt. Do you hear me? Promise me you won't call him…and you won't get anybody else to do it, either. Promise, or I'm telling Jon you're allergic to flowers."

Carolina sighed. "Oh, all right, I promise. But you have to tell him sooner or later. Kurt, I mean. Jon *knows* how I feel about getting flowers." A secret smile settled on her lips, and as if on cue, her cell phone rang. "Ah, speak of the devil," she said. "I'll take this outside. Bye, Emily. And take my advice. Get some crackers." With a wave of her hand, she swept out of the house as gracefully as she'd swept in, pressing the tiny cell phone to her ear, tossing her braids, saying into the phone, "I thought I told you never to speak to me again."

Emily watched from the doorway, wondering how

she and Carolina could possibly share the same genetic material. *If you want him, go get him,* Carolina had said as if it were the obvious solution. Could it possibly be that simple? Emily thought. Could she simply decide she wanted Kurt and go after him? Could she choose to believe their marriage would work and make it happen? Could she tell Kurt she loved him and expect him to love her in return? Was that settling for second best?

*Yes, yes, yes, and...no.* Whatever the past had held for Carolina and Kurt, it was past. Whatever the future held for Kurt and Emily was still out there, their ending not yet written, the possibilities still theirs for the asking. So why shouldn't she ask? And expect Kurt to rise to the challenge? As unbelievable as it had seemed yesterday, Emily blithely, confidently decided he did love her. And she would tell him so.

Just as soon as her stomach stopped roiling.

THE STUNT called for Hank to pick up the straw hat and set it on the hero's head, but the horse was in no mood to follow the movie script, and he dropped the hat into the water trough, instead. ''For Pete's sake, Hank,'' Kurt exclaimed, picking up the dripping Stetson and trying to slap the water off it. ''Can't you get this right just once?''

Shaking his magnificent head, the stallion trotted to the far side of the corral and eyed Kurt with stubborn resistence, all but stating out loud that it wasn't *his* fault Emily had left them. Which was true. Twenty-four hours after she'd left, Kurt still didn't know where the fault lay. He didn't know why Emily had left. He didn't know when she'd packed her things and driven away in the Mustang. He just knew she'd slipped out of the bet, the bed and his arms at some time during the night, leaving him to awaken alone and so lonely he'd felt like wailing at the moon. Except the moon was long gone, too.

In the distress of finding she'd left him, Kurt had discovered her cryptic note. ''Uncle!'' she'd written, as if that were an explanation. And the very sight of the single defeated word made Kurt mad. Worse than mad. She'd made a fool out of him. Just as he'd decided she was nothing like Carolina, Emily had conned him into falling flat on his face in love with her and then walked out. To prove what? That she had as little respect for a man's tender emotions as her sister did? That she could bring a man to his knees and then squash his pride flat with her indifference? That she could get him to cry uncle while she walked away with his heart in her pocket?

Well, goodbye and good riddance. It'd be a cold day in hell before he let a Dawson anywhere near him again. Drunk or sober, he'd stay as far away from Emily as it was possible to get. And he'd make damn certain she didn't get to use his name for any purpose after the annulment, either. It was small retribution, but he figured she owed him at least that much out of this fiasco of a marriage.

The sound of a sports car roaring up the drive brought a snort of disapproval from Hank and a round of frenzied barking from Melba. Not bothering to close the gate behind him, Kurt stepped out of the corral to see who was coming and had to fight a wave of disappointment when he realized it wasn't Emily. The car was sleek, black, and purred to a stop right in front of him. When Carolina pushed open the door and stepped out, all Kurt felt was annoyance at the dust she'd stirred up. Then he looked at her—perused the beautiful face, the pouty lips, the seductive smile, the magnificent body—and wondered what in hell she had done to her hair. "Hello, Carolina," was all he cared enough to say. "Long time, no see."

"Well, it wasn't me who stayed away." She gave her head a toss that once he might have found enchanting, but that now just clattered in an irritating clink of beaded braids. "I got tired of waiting for you, Kurt, so I married someone else."

"Congratulations," he said, and realized he meant it. "I married someone else, too."

Her lips tightened, but she still had the market cornered on saucy smiles. "Don't think I'm going to forgive you for involving Emily in this shameful business, Kurt, because I won't. You could have married any other woman in this town, and I would have wished you happy. But you had to go and marry my sister on the rebound, and I just flat am not going to forgive you for it.''

Kurt smiled, if only because she was so majestically sure that the world revolved around her. ''I didn't marry her on the rebound,'' he said. ''I happen to have fallen in love with Emily.''

Carolina tossed those wimpy braids again. ''Maybe you did,'' she said sweetly. ''Or maybe you married her because you were drunk as a skunk. I've heard the whole sordid story, Kurt, so there's no need to lie. You were brokenhearted over my marriage to Jon. The whole town's talking about it. Even Emily knows why you married her.''

If there had been scars from that broken heart, Kurt couldn't find any evidence of them now. Standing there, facing the woman he once thought he'd love his whole life long, Kurt realized how lucky—how damn lucky—he was to be free of her. She could, and would, believe he'd go to his grave still in love with her, but he knew now that whatever he'd felt for her had died a natural death a long time ago. Otherwise, he would have married her years before and taken no chances that she'd ever leave him. As Emily had.

''You've been to see Emily, I take it?'' he asked, because he was hungry for news of her and he didn't really care if Carolina knew it.

''I came home from my honeymoon early just to

be with her. I've just come from her house, in fact. She looks awful and feels worse. You should be ashamed of yourself.''

''Me? She's the one who walked out.''

Carolina sighed dramatically, as if she couldn't believe what fools men could be. ''Of course she did, you idiot. She's known for years that you were in love with me, then you go and marry her because you think she *is* me, and she knows you're so stubborn you'll insist on *staying* married to her just because of the baby. I hated to do it, but I told her she was right. The whole town knows how you feel about—''

''Baby?'' Kurt said slowly. ''What baby?''

Carolina reached out to touch his arm, but Melba growled a warning. ''I see you still have that nasty little dog,'' she said, and Melba started barking again.

Kurt ignored the dog and the barking and the disgusted look on Carolina's face and tried not to encourage the sudden faint glow of hope inside his heart. ''What baby?'' he repeated.

Carolina shrugged. ''Emily's pregnant. She swears she's not, but I know the symptoms. She can claim it's an upset stomach until she's blue in the face, I know better.''

''But she can't be—'' Kurt did some quick math in his head, even factoring in the possibility that she hadn't been lying about their wedding night, and still came up short. "I mean, how could she even know so early in the—" He shook his head. "This is some kind of game with the two of you, isn't it? Some kind of sick joke."

"She's sick, all right." Carolina stepped against the car as Hank came closer, maybe just looking for strawberries, but then again, maybe not. "Mom got sick immediately when she was pregnant with Em. She didn't have to go to the doctor to know what her condition was, and Emily's the same. She probably got pregnant on your wedding night—honestly, Kurt, I can't believe you took advantage of her like that—but she doesn't want you to know about this because obviously she doesn't want to stay married to you even if you are the father of her baby."

Kurt did the math again and came up with several interesting possibilities—all of them centering around the idea that Emily was going to have his baby. His baby. His wife. His whole life. And he wasn't going to stand by and lose them. No matter what he had to do to convince Emily that their marriage of mishaps had been made in heaven from the start.

"Where is she?" He was already moving toward the car, reaching out to take the keys from Carolina's hands.

"At her house," Carolina said, closing her fist on the keys. "Sick as a dog and nursing a broken heart, thanks to you. But don't think I'm going to drive you there, because I won't. I'm driving to the airport to pick up my husband.''

Kurt looked from the car to the other immediate means of transportation. ''Then I'll do it the cowboy way,'' he said, and swung onto Hank's back. To hell with the insurance company, he thought, and with Melba racing beside them, he rode hell-bent for leather toward town.

KURT DIDN'T even knock. He burst into the room like a bat out of hell, followed by a panting Melba, who collapsed on the floor like a rag dog. Emily looked from the terrier to the brown paper sack in Kurt's hands, and the only thought to come readily to mind was the hope that he hadn't brought her saltine crackers. He looked at her, sprawled on the sofa in tousled sweatpants and a rumpled T-shirt. Her hair had been jerked into a limp ponytail, her makeup hadn't even made it out of the drawer, much less onto her face. She had probably never looked worse in her life.

So much for following her first impulse to fling herself into his arms and explain to him that he was, in fact, crazy in love with her. Most likely, that would have him throwing up, too. ''What have you done to this dog?'' she asked. ''She looks exhausted.''

''She and Hank needed a little exercise. She'll be

fine." Kurt's eyes narrowed on her pale face. "I'm not so sure about you."

"Let me guess," Emily said with fatal certainty as she swung her legs to the floor and sat up. "Carolina called you."

"No," Kurt said, anger so tight in his voice he almost sounded like a tenor instead of a baritone. "She came to see me."

Emily should have guessed that was the way Carolina would get around her promise. "I knew she couldn't stay out of this."

"She said you didn't want me to know."

"You can always count on Carolina to keep her promises." Emily peeked at him, glad he was here, no matter who, what, where or why. He'd pushed back his hat, and the mark of it still creased his forehead. His eyes were stormy. There was a streak of dirt on his cheek, and he smelled like horses and the stable. He looked dusty, furious, frantic...and she loved him so much her heart was practically panting with excitement. "If you came for the car, the key's on the kitchen table."

"I came because you're pregnant and I'm the father."

Emily laughed, feeling nervous and hopeful and anticipating an argument. "I'm not pregnant," she said simply.

"Carolina said you are."

"She said wrong."

"She said you'd deny it, too."

Emily sighed. "I'm not denying it, Kurt. There's nothing to deny. I'm not pregnant."

He dumped the contents of the paper bag onto the table, causing Melba to sit up and take notice. "Prove it," he said.

Astounded, Emily leaned forward and scratched the terrier's head as she read the labels on the scattered boxes. Early Bird Pregnancy Test. First Indicator Pregnancy Test. Be Sure—For the woman who needs to know now! On the Spot Home Pregnancy Kit. Proof Positive... When Every Minute Counts. And one generic box with nothing more than Pregnancy Kit above the printed directions. She swallowed a nervous giggle and looked at Kurt. "There must be a dozen of these," she said. "How much proof do you need?"

"Nellis said they sometimes give a false negative."

Emily blinked. "You took Nellis with you to shop for pregnancy tests?"

"Somebody had to hold onto Hank for me while I was in the drugstore."

"H—Hank? What was your horse doing at the drugstore?"

Kurt's jaw tightened, but he managed not to look embarrassed. "I rode him into town," he said with an offhand shrug. "It was faster than finding Ray and getting my hands on the truck. Probably not the smartest thing I've ever done, but I was in a hurry.''

''I thought you didn't use Hank for ordinary things like a trip into town.''

''This isn't any ordinary trip into town,'' he said, although that fact was painfully obvious. ''And Hank's no worse for the wear. He's outside now, with Nellis and a quart of strawberries.''

Emily walked slowly to the window to see that Hank and Nellis were, indeed, on her front lawn. So much for the hope her condition wouldn't become general knowledge. Rumors were undoubtedly zipping from Main Street to the interstate and back. She couldn't even *not* get pregnant without burning down the town grapevine. She lifted her hand in a resigned wave. ''Maybe we should just invite Nellis to come on in,'' she said.

''He's busy,'' Kurt said sharply. ''What I want to know is why I had to hear about this from your sister.''

''Because she doesn't have the good sense to mind her own business?''

''Carolina has never had any interest in minding anyone's business but her own,'' he said, showing that he knew the woman better than one might have expected. ''I haven't been able to think of a single reason she'd tell me this unless it were true. So...'' His hand made a sweeping gesture above the boxes. ''Pick one and let's get started.''

Emily couldn't believe he was serious. "Kurt, listen to me. I am not pregnant. If there was even a remote possibility that I could be, I'd tell you. But there isn't. And I'm not."

He stooped, putting the coffee table and the pile of boxes between them, and he regarded her with a gaze both frustrated and tender. "I know it's unusual to know immediately, but Carolina said your mother got sick right away when she was pregnant with you. And there is more than a remote possibility, Emily. We did have intercourse."

"And we did use condoms."

"One could have broken. It is possible."

"Yes, and it *is* possible that I know I only have an upset stomach."

"Carolina said you'd say that."

"Carolina is an idiot. Even if she is my sister."

He picked up one of the boxes and held it out to her. "You can't keep something like this to yourself, Emily. You don't have to. And don't go thinking I'll run off and leave you to raise the baby by yourself, either. I'll take care of you. You can count on that."

She would have loved to tell him she knew he would make a wonderful father. She would have loved to tell him she wanted nothing more than for him to take care of her. She would have loved for him to believe her and not Carolina. "Give me that." Snatching the box from his hand, she got up and walked irritably to the bathroom.

KURT couldn't believe how happy he was when the test turned up positive.

"I told you so." Emily was not happy with him, and it showed. "I told you it was just an upset stomach."

"You told me it was impossible," he said, looking at the results spread out on the bathroom counter. "So why is this test positive?"

"It's a false positive, Kurt. False. One positive. Eleven negatives. You do the math."

"Easy. One in twelve says you are."

"And the other eleven say I'm not. Even you aren't idiot enough to bet on those odds, Kurtis."

"You want to wager a little something on that, darlin'?"

"Are you crazy?"

"No," he said stubbornly, wondering why he couldn't stop arguing with her, why he couldn't just accept the results and be glad Emily wasn't going to be in his life for the rest of his life. "I'm convinced this test is right and the others are wrong, and I'm calling the doctor right now to make you an appointment for Monday morning."

"You go near that phone and I will personally see that you never touch-tone again!"

She was really hot—angry hot—and he knew he

was acting like a fool. But he couldn't quite give up the idea that she was pregnant with his baby. He wanted to watch Emily grow round with maternity, watch her nurse and nurture a son. Or daughter. "Look, Emily, I just need to know if it's true. I just want…to know."

Her eyes searched his, clearly mystified by his insistence. "Well, I want to know what's wrong with you, Kurt. Most men would be ecstatic to know they've escaped a close call with parenthood. You, especially. But you're acting like you're disappointed."

He was. From the moment Carolina had told him Emily was pregnant, he'd been making plans. He'd go get her, bring her home, they'd tell Cousin Milton to forget the annulment and make sure their marriage was legally as solid as the Hoover Dam. Kurt's kid was never going to wonder if his parents had been married to make him legitimate. No, sir. His son would know from the start that the marriage came first. Children needed to know things like that. He'd decided on the way into town that he'd ask one of the other trainers to take Hank on the upcoming location job. Kurt didn't want to take any chance on being away from home if the baby happened to come early. He'd mentally sketched out an addition to the house already, too. A nursery.

Kurt looked at Emily, all flushed and mad and pretty, and thought what an idiot he was. She wasn't hanging on to that one chance in twelve. She'd only done all the tests at his insistence. She wasn't disappointed. Hell, why would she be? She'd made it clear she had no interest in making a life with him. Winning the bet had been her only reason for seducing him. The fact that she'd lost the bet bothered him only for a second. Like as not, she'd figured out a way to turn it around so she won by default or something. "I'm taking the car," he said, ready to fight her all the way to the stick shift for custody. "Don't think I won't."

The flush of anger receded in her cheeks. "I figured you'd come for it sometime."

"You're danged right. I won this bet fair and square, and I want to hear you say it."

"You won the bet fair and square," she said.

He'd expected some fire, a token protest, at least. "I didn't hear the magic word," he prompted, knowing that he would kiss her long and hard before he'd let the word *uncle* pass those lips. "Come on, Emily. You're not too chicken to *say* it, are you?"

Sure enough, her chin came up, and that familiar, wonderful, earthy fire sparked in her eyes. "I left you a note," she said.

"Melba ate it. I never even got to read it."

"You're lying."

"Maybe. Maybe not."

"Maybe you should just get on your horse right now and go home."

He knew suddenly that he wasn't leaving this house without her. No matter what. "Not until you tell me what I want to hear."

"I'm not telling you another blessed thing, McCauley. I said you won the bet, I told you I'm not pregnant and I told you I'd give you the car. I don't have anything else to say to you."

"*Give* me the car?" He latched onto her phrasing like a man with a mission. "Those sound like fighting words to me."

"Fine," she said, the color rising again in her cheeks. "I'm keeping the car. So there. And if by some bizarre stroke of bad luck that one test in twelve is right, I'm keeping the baby, too."

He reached for her, grasping her shoulders forcefully. "Well, while you're at it, maybe you think you can just keep my name, too. Sew it on those blasted khaki pants no matter what I might have to say about it."

"Good idea, Kurtis. Thanks, I think I will."

His heart pounded his rib cage just like it did in the few seconds before the rodeo chute would open and the bucking bronc would break loose beneath him. Those had been the rides of his life until he'd pulled back that shower curtain and seen Emily. She was the only challenge he wanted from here on out. About all the challenge any man ever needed to tackle. "You're welcome," he said, quieter, with more hope than he'd ever risked in his life.

She blinked, looked at him. "I am?"

He nodded, afraid that she wouldn't...afraid that she didn't...afraid he could still lose the best wife he'd ever happened to marry. "You're welcome to use my name, pet my dog, ride my horse, drive my car, have my baby...there's just one catch."

She frowned. "Do I have to say uncle?"

"I love you," he said, realizing that was what this had been about from the beginning.

"I love you?" she whispered, her eyes widening as he pulled her closer to him.

"No, Emily. I love you. Say it like that. Not like a question."

"I love you," she repeated obediently, a smile beginning on her lips.

"Now say it like you mean it."

"I love you." She tried again.

"Better, but try it once more." His heart was never going to be able to pass this endurance test, he thought. But something in her gaze told him to have faith. "Like this—I love you."

"That *sounds* like you meant it," she agreed.

"What would you say if I told you I did mean it?"

She swallowed hard. "Hot damn?"

God almighty, he loved her. "Listen up, woman, this is the way it's gonna be from now on. We're married and we're staying married. And the next time we take a pregnancy test, it'd better be eleven to one positive. Plus, you will not be wearing anything but a towel in the bedroom for the next fifty or so years. Got it?''

She nodded meekly. ''What are you going to be wearing?''

''A big cowboy smile.''

''Hm,'' she said. ''Before this goes any further, McCauley, I think you need to repeat after me, 'I will spend the next fifty—or so—years thanking the guardian angel of lonesome cowboys for guiding me to this smart, savvy—''

''—beautiful,'' he interjected.

''—intelligent woman—''

''—with really great legs—''

''—who I don't deserve—''

''Whoa. Back up there,'' he said.

''Oh, come on, McCauley, you know how lucky you are that it was me you married and not... someone else.''

''Carolina, for instance?''

Emily met his gaze, and he wanted to kiss her so much he ached with it. ''I was an idiot not to see that you were the best of the litter. Let me make it up to you. Starting now, ending maybe fifty years or so.''

''Starting now?'' she asked. ''What about Nellis and Hank? You can't just leave them outside by themselves wondering what we're doing in here.

You can't even begin to make up with me while Melba's sitting right outside the door.''

"Nellis has probably already loaded Hank in a trailer and headed for the ranch. At least, that's what I told him to do if I wasn't back in twenty minutes. And Melba is just going to have to accept the fact that I'm crazy in love with my wife.''

"Pretty sure of yourself, aren't you, cowboy?'' She began unbuttoning his shirt.

"Not really,'' he said, getting distracted by her busy fingers. "What are you doing?''

"Well, first I'm going to undress you,'' she said. "Then you're going to undress me.''

"I like that part,'' he said, reaching for the tie of her sweatpants.

"Then we're going to take a shower and you're going to scrub my back and I'm going to—''

"—scrub my front.''

"—and then we're going to lock the door of the bedroom so Melba won't be scarred for life, turn off the phone and get into bed.''

"Promise you won't drive off in my Mustang in the middle of the night?'' He began kissing the sweet hollow of her neck.

"Not as long as you keep kissing me like that,'' she said on a sigh of pure delight.

"You can count on it.'' He kissed her neck, her lips, her ears and all the hollows in between. "But what are the people of this town going to think when we don't come out of this bedroom for the next fifty years...or so?"

She looped her arms around his neck and pulled him seductively closer. "Well, whatever wild, passionate, crazy, fantastic lovemaking they can imagine is actually happening behind our closed doors...for once, they'll be right." She kissed him then, long and lustily, and he knew for a fact that he was the luckiest cowboy on God's green earth and in the whole great state of Nevada.

Possibly even in Nova Scotia.

# Rebellious, bold and... a father!

## THE AUSTRALIANS

Stories of romance Australian-style, guaranteed to
fulfill that sense of adventure!

This May 1999 look for

# *Taming a Husband*
## by Elizabeth Duke

Jake Thorn has never been one to settle down. He couldn't
stay with Lexie, even though his heart yearned to, and he
struck out across the continent before she could tell the
daddy-to-be the big news. Now, determined to give love
another chance, Jake has returned—and is shocked to find
himself a father!

*The Wonder from Down Under: where spirited women win
the hearts of Australia's most independent men!*

Available May 1999
at your favorite retail outlet.

## HARLEQUIN®
*Makes any time special* ™

PHAUS11